MW00988018

LONE STAR PROTECTOR

Delores Fossen

Lone Star Books

Copyright © 2024 Delores Fossen

All rights reserved

The characters and events portrayed in this book are
fictitious. Any similarity to real persons, living or dead, is
coincidental and not intended by the author.

No part of this book may be reproduced, or stored in a
retrieval system, or transmitted in any form or by any
means, electronic, mechanical, photocopying, recording,
or otherwise, without express written permission of the
publisher.

ISBN-13: 9798876892676

Cover design by: Danielle Ness
Library of Congress Control Number: 2018675309
Printed in the United States of America

For Charra, Clinton, Justin, and Beth.
You've given me headaches, worry lines
and so very much happiness and joy.
You'll always, always be my babies.

CONTENTS

CHAPTER ONE

——— ☆ ———

Nash McKenna drove as if his life depended on it. Or rather as if *her* life depended on it. Because it sure as hell did. She could be dying right now.

Caroline.

He tried to shut out the images of her being attacked. And failed big time. So, he just kept up the bat out of hell pace, speeding toward her place in the Texas Hill Country.

Normally, this would have been a scenic trip, threading his SUV past the chalk-white bluffs, the clear water creeks, the mineral springs, and the fields crammed with spring wildflowers. There was no way for him to enjoy the view now though. Not when there was so much at stake.

He had to get to Caroline before the killer did.

Had to.

His phone vibrated, and like the other messages he'd received in the past ten minutes, this one immediately loaded on his dash monitor. "Status?" he muttered, saying the single word of the text aloud.

The question was from his boss, Ruby

Maverick, head of Maverick Ops, an elite team of former military and law enforcement officers who handled everything from life and death investigations to personal security services.

In this case, the *personal* applied. Man, did it.

Because Caroline was Ruby's daughter.

Caroline was other things, too. Again, personal stuff. But Nash couldn't think of that now either. He just kept driving and took yet another turn that would get him closer to her.

"Reply to text," he instructed his AI program that he recently renamed Oz for the movie that'd had both entertained and scared the crap out of him when he'd been a kid. "I'm two minutes out from Caroline's place."

One hundred and twenty seconds wasn't that long, but it would likely feel like a lifetime or two to the normally unflappable Ruby. To say things were strained between Caroline and her was like saying the ocean had a drop or two of water in it. Still, Ruby loved her daughter, and this threat had to be clawing away at her.

Ruby would have no doubt wanted to make this trip herself, but she was hours away on a business trip in Austin. Nash had just returned from an assignment and had been at his place. Since that put him only about twenty miles from Caroline's, he'd been the one Ruby had tapped to come after Caroline hadn't responded to multiple phone calls and texts.

Nash had sent some of those texts to her. He'd

made a couple of calls, too, that had gone straight to voicemail. Normally, that wouldn't have made him curse a blue streak. Or get twisted up with worry. Then again, he didn't normally make a habit of calling Caroline, but this was nowhere close to a normal situation.

The county cops were on the way to her house, too, but they had been even further out than Nash. Added to that, the dispatcher had apparently told Ruby they were short-staffed and would be sending out only one deputy.

No way had Ruby wanted to trust her daughter's safety to a single cop. Hell, she would have probably sent out an entire platoon or police squad if she could have managed it.

Nash felt a little relief when he saw Caroline's mailbox. Her address was on the side, and it had a small red, orange, and purple sculpture on top.

A phoenix.

He knew it was the name of Caroline's blown glass studio. A studio that just about everybody, including him, considered to be the textbook definition of out in the sticks. She was a good half mile from her nearest neighbor, and while he normally didn't consider that a bad thing, he did right now.

There'd be no one to hear her scream.

No one to come running to try to help her.

That gave Nash a vicious gut punch feeling and added a spike to the urgency building inside him that in no way needed more spikes. The urgency

3

was already sky-high and bordering on panic.

Her house *finally* came into view. It was snuggled in between a bunch of trees and a pasture with a pond. The house itself was small, one story, white, with dark green shutters. But the building next to it was the size of a barn.

Caroline's work studio.

That's where he parked, and the tires skidded to a stop over the loose gravel surface. Nash immediately drew his Glock, bolted from his SUV, and raced toward the door of the studio. He yanked it hard enough to cause the muscles in his shoulder to protest, and then he cursed.

Because it was locked.

"Caroline?" he called out.

Yeah, he was loud enough to give away his location to a killer, but he'd already done that with his not so quiet approach. He wasn't going for stealth here. He was racing against the clock to save her.

"Caroline?" he shouted again.

There was still no answer so he used his fist to pound on the door. And pound. When that got him no response, he moved back, ready to ram into it until it gave way. Before he could do that though, the door opened.

And there she was.

Caroline.

"What the heck do you want?" she snarled before she even got a look at him. "I'm working."

Her face was beaded with sweat, and she had

a red bandana headband holding back her short blonde hair. Her amber eyes were narrowed to slits.

Nash could see now that she was indeed working. Or better yet, he could feel it. The furnace she used to melt glass was chugging out a blistering heat that rushed right out at him. But something else rushed out at him, too.

Relief.

God. So much relief.

Nash nearly grabbed her and hauled her into his arms. Not the first time he'd had that urge, but those other occasions had been when he'd wanted her so bad that it'd hurt. But now, it was all about seeing that she was alive, that she hadn't been sliced to pieces by a killer.

"Nash," Caroline muttered, and some of the annoyance and anger slipped from her voice and her expression when she no doubt noticed the look he was giving her. "What happened? Why are you here?"

Both good questions, especially since he didn't make a habit of visiting her. Or being around her.

Too much temptation.

After all, she was the boss' daughter, and that made Caroline the kind of forbidden attraction that could get his ass fired the hard way. Even though there'd been times when he would have risked that if… well, just *if*.

The stars definitely weren't aligned when it came to Caroline and him.

Since he knew Ruby would be more than eager for an update, Nash fired off a quick text to let his boss know that he'd made it to Caroline's and, more importantly, that she was all right and that there were no signs of a killer.

Ruby's response came within seconds. "Stay with her until you hear from me."

While the text seemed composed enough, Nash figured Ruby was having her own extreme relief reaction right now.

Caroline glanced at his phone, then she took out hers from her pocket. Peering down at her screen, she no doubt saw the missed messages and texts. Obviously, she'd either silenced it or simply hadn't responded since she'd been working.

She locked gazes with him. "Just say it fast," she insisted. "Is it my mother? Did something happen to her?"

"It's Bodie," he managed to say once he got his throat unclamped.

She flinched. Of course, she did. Flinched and dropped back a step. That's when her gaze slid to his hand.

To his gun.

"He escaped from prison?" she asked.

Nash nodded. "Yeah, Bodie escaped."

He couldn't use the term, *my brother*, but that's exactly what Bodie was. An asshole bastard who happened to share some DNA with Nash.

But Bodie was a whole lot more than that.

He was also the man who'd left Caroline for

dead nearly eighteen years ago when she'd been a college freshman, ready to start her adult life.

A life that Bodie had come so damn close to ending.

She swallowed hard, and since she looked ready to drop where she stood, he reached out to stop her from falling. No falling though. In a move that surprised him, Caroline whipped out a knife in a leather case from the pocket of her cargo pants. A big assed knife that she unsheathed in a blink. She held it up so the afternoon sunlight glinted off the eight-inch blade.

"He's coming here for me?" she asked, her voice a little wobbly.

Again, Nash had to nod, and it crushed him to confirm that. Crushed him even more to see the fear that put in her eyes.

"Bodie escaped late last night when he was in the infirmary," Nash explained. He'd spare her the details of how Bodie had throat-punched a male nurse and used the nurse's ID and vehicle to get away. "The last sighting was from a traffic camera on the Interstate. He took the exit to your place."

Of course, that exit was a good ten miles from Caroline's house, but there was that whole "off the beaten path" thing. Caroline's wasn't near a city where Bodie could blend in and disappear. There were no nearby stores or places for him to get supplies and regroup. There'd be only one reason for Bodie to use that route.

To come after Caroline again.

To try to do what he'd nearly managed when she'd been just eighteen.

To try to kill her.

He'd come damn close the first time, leaving her with eleven stab wounds and in a puddle of her own blood. The only reason she'd lived was because her dorm mate had come home early from a date and had walked in on the carnage. The date, a football player on scholarship, had been with the roommate, and he'd managed to knock Bodie unconscious so he could then be arrested.

And so Caroline could be taken to the hospital.

Where she'd stayed for three months, four days, and sixteen hours.

Time when Nash had done a lot praying that she would recover. Time he'd also spent cursing his so-called brother.

"Did my mother send you?" she asked. But Caroline waved that off. "Of course, she sent you. So, what do we do? Do we just wait for him to show up?"

The answer to that was yes. But again, he didn't spell it out. "If he comes, I *will* bury him."

Nash hadn't meant to use the tone of a cold-blooded killer, but he hadn't been able to yank back his gut reaction.

Caroline had an odd reaction, too. She smiled. It wasn't a big one, and it was laced with nerves. But it was there all right.

"You'll bury him if I don't beat you to it," she assured him. "I'm not a defenseless eighteen-year-old girl any longer. I'm a thirty-six-year-old woman with a black belt in Taekwondo who's had extensive training in hand-to-hand combat, firearms, and these."

She held up the knife again, and in a move that stunned him, she turned and hurled it toward a wood target that had been fixed to the wall. The target had the outline of a man painted on it, and her knife speared it right in the area where the heart would be.

"I'll cut him to ribbons if he gets near me," she added, going to the knife and yanking it out so she could re-sheath it.

Nash had a bittersweet reaction. He was glad Caroline could defend herself. So damn glad that she hadn't let the attack beat her down. But he hated she had lost a part of herself that she'd never get back.

Hated even more that her world had just turned upside down.

Again.

He had to tell her that they needed to go inside, just in case Bodie had managed to get his hand on a gun and was at this moment taking aim at her. And Nash knew Bodie was a good shot, too. That'd come from being raised in a compound with preppers and survivalists as parents and neighbors. Like Nash and his other two brothers, Bodie had learned to hunt and shoot before he'd gotten out of elementary school.

Nash was about to get her moving inside when

the sound shot through the barn. His first thought was that it was gunfire. But it wasn't.

He looked past her shoulder to see the concrete floor covered with glass. Caroline groaned, muttered some profanity under her breath, and went closer to look down at the mess.

"This is what happens when a piece cools too fast." Caroline sighed, and then did more cursing. "I was about to get it in an annealing oven when you banged on the door."

"What was it before it broke?" he asked, closing the door behind him and locking it. It was seriously hot in the studio, but it was better to risk heat exhaustion than a bullet to the head.

"A tropical ocean wave at sunrise. A commissioned piece," Caroline added in a mutter.

Nash would never admit it to her, but he'd done some research on her and knew her commissioned art earned her a six-figure-plus living. And from what he could see of the glistening shards of blue, green, and gold, this creation would have been up to her usual beautiful standards.

Like some of the other pieces in the room.

He glanced around at the shelves stuffed with all sorts of glass sculptures, vases, and bowls. Again, he knew that some of them would be going to gift shops in San Antonio and Austin. Others would be shipped all over the world.

Caroline stood there, her back to him, staring at the ruined sculpture. Even now, when things seemed to be racing to the hell in a handbasket arena, he could feel the heat.

The lust.

Yeah, that was it. Lust. Probably because of the forbidden part playing into it. But he thought maybe it was something that went deeper than that. All the way to the marrow of his bones.

He'd felt it the first time he'd laid eyes on Caroline.

She hadn't been standing then but had rather been in a hospital bed. Six weeks into that three month and four day stay. Nash had been about to head out on his first deployment as an Air Force Combat Rescue Officer, but he'd made a detour to the hospital to try to tell Caroline just how sorry he was that his dick of a brother had done this to her.

Nash hadn't gotten past the door.

He'd seen her sleeping. Just lying there. So beautiful. Still so damaged and recovering from her most recent surgery. He'd stood there, silently cursing what'd happened to her.

Silently cursing the lust, too.

After all, he'd been twenty-three. A big age gap, considering Caroline had been just eighteen. But even that wasn't the biggest obstacle. No. Not when his brother had come so close to ending her life.

Nash had been contemplating that. His dick brother. Her injuries. Her amazing face. And the lust.

When Ruby had stepped up beside him.

Because Nash had researched Caroline, he'd

also known who Ruby was. A lieutenant colonel in the Army. Former special ops. All hard-assed. And she had *advised* Nash that now wasn't a good time to spill his apology. Ruby and he had been discussing that when Caroline had woken up and asked who he was. After Nash had drawn in enough air to speak, he'd told her.

Caroline had been more than civil, but he'd also seen the wariness in her eyes. Even though he didn't have a close resemblance to Bodie, they did have the same black hair, the same build. That must have given her flashbacks from hell.

And it was the reason he'd avoided her from then on.

The avoidance had lasted until three years ago when Caroline had run into him at a Christmas party. Nash and she had talked. Even danced. And he was certain she'd felt the same pull of heat that he had.

Certain, too, that she had put up an equal resistance.

There was some of that resistance in her now as she turned toward him. "Is Bodie still obsessed with me?"

That was a good word for it. *Obsession*. Caroline had gone out with Bodie once, but after she'd declined another date with him, he'd stalked her. Harassed her. Terrified her.

And then tried to kill her.

"I haven't had any contact with Bodie for years," he replied. "I went to see him in prison after…afterwards," Nash settled for saying. He'd wanted to know why Bodie had done it.

Nash had gotten an answer he'd take the grave.

Because if I can't have her, no one else will. No one. Caroline is mine.

A sick asshole response from a sick obsessed asshole, but Nash had no idea if Bodie still felt the same way. Considering the exit Bodie had taken, Nash was thinking the answer was yes.

"Have you had any contact with him?" Nash asked her.

She shook her head, peeled off the bandana, and repeated the headshake. "Thankfully, he wasn't allowed to send me letters, emails or such."

The words had barely left her mouth when Nash heard something. The sound of a car engine, and it was making a fast approach toward them. He didn't have to draw his gun since he was already holding it.

"Move back," he told Caroline, and he made sure it wasn't a request but rather an order.

Did she listen?

Of course not.

She was right next to Nash when he hurried to the door. Since there were no windows or even a peephole, he eased open the door, hoping he'd see Ruby or one of his Maverick Ops teammates.

But it wasn't.

The sleek silver Mercedes skidded to a stop next to his SUV, and someone hurried out. Not Bodie. This was a tall brunette that Nash didn't recognize.

Nash couldn't see if she was armed, but he stepped in front of Caroline anyway. "Who are you and what do you want?" he demanded.

The woman ignored him, instead pinning her attention over his shoulder and directly on Caroline. "Where's Bodie?" she shouted. "What the hell have you done with him?"

CHAPTER TWO

——————— ☆ ———————

Apparently, this was going to be a day of surprises, but Caroline hoped this visitor, this stranger, wasn't as nasty of a surprise as the one Nash had already doled out.

That Bodie had escaped.

And that he was likely on his way to kill her.

This woman obviously didn't think that though. In fact, judging from her second question, she appeared to believe Caroline was the one in control here, that she was somehow after Bodie.

Not totally off the mark.

Caroline had already made up her mind that this time she'd be ready for the sonofabitch. This time, she wouldn't have her back turned to him. This time, she would see the attack coming. This time, she wouldn't be eighteen years old and way too trusting. She'd face him head on and make him pay for what he'd done to her.

Of course, Nash might have the same idea in mind.

That was why he kept moving in front of her despite Bodie being nowhere in sight. However, she supposed this woman, whoever the heck she was, could be just as much of a threat.

"Who are you, and what do you want?" Nash repeated, and he sounded more than a little dangerous.

Looked it, too.

He'd probably just come from an op because he was wearing dark camo pants, combat boots, and a black tee that showed off all those incredible muscles. Something she probably shouldn't be noticing at a time like this, but she would have been blind not to have seen them. As her crusty granny would have said—the man was built like a brick shithouse.

The woman shifted her attention to Nash, dismissing him with an annoyed flick of a glance before looking at Caroline again. "Where's Bodie?" she yelled. "You'd better not have hurt him, you bitch."

Caroline huffed. "Listen, *bitch*," she fired right back. Her days of backing down from a fight were long over. "I haven't hurt Bodie. I haven't even seen the piece of shit. What makes you think I have?"

The woman snapped back her shoulders and seemed to rethink what she'd been about to spew. "You're lying," she muttered, and she repeated that a couple of times before she sagged against her car. It was as if her legs had given out on her.

"I'm not lying, and you'd better tell me who you are right now," Caroline demanded.

"I'm Jordana McKenna," she said, the fire no

longer blazing her voice or her expression. She looked defeated.

"McKenna?" Nash and Caroline questioned in unison. It was a toss-up as to who was more shocked and confused by that.

Since McKenna was Nash's surname.

And Bodie's.

"Oz, do a search on Jordana McKenna," Nash instructed without taking his eyes off their visitor.

Caroline figured he was talking to his AI app that was a staple among her mother's operatives. She got confirmation of that when his phone began doling out some details.

"Jordana McKenna, nee Harris. Married to Bodie McKenna for four months and one week."

"Oz, pause," Nash said, and he made a sound of disgust while he popped in an earbud. "You married a convicted felon?" There was plenty of disgust in his voice, too, when he asked that of their visitor.

Jordana's chin whipped up. "I married a man I love. A man who loves me. And he was wrongfully convicted."

"Beg to differ on that last part, and I've got the scars to prove it," Caroline muttered.

She saw Nash flinch just a little and understood it hurt for him to be reminded of what his brother had done. It didn't matter that Nash hadn't been part of the attack, and he sure as heck hadn't condoned it. It also didn't matter either that he'd basically disowned Bodie before that godawful night. Nash still felt responsible, maybe believing he could have done something to stop it even though he hadn't been within a thousand miles of the attack.

Later, Caroline would tell him that she didn't blame him. But for now, she had to deal with his *sister-in-law*. A woman who was possibly delusional. Then again, she'd heard of other seemingly stable women marrying inmates.

"You lied to the police about your so-called attack," Jordana insisted. "That's why Bodie went to jail."

All right, maybe not unstable, but rather gullible to believe a man who was behind bars for attempted murder. Caroline didn't bother to try to set her straight, but she wondered how *Mrs. McKenna* would react if she hiked up her top and showed her the thirteen scars from the stab wounds on her torso.

While she was debating doing just that, Caroline heard the wail of a police siren in the distance. So, the cavalry was on the way. Probably her mother, too, and it twisted at her to think that her place, her sanctuary, would soon be crawling with people.

Maybe one of them a would-be killer.

"Where is Bodie?" Jordana repeated.

"You tell me," Caroline countered. "What makes you think he would come here? I mean, since you don't believe he tried to murder me."

The woman's mouth tightened. "He might feel

as if he has to settle an old score with you."

"Right," Caroline muttered. "Wonder how many times he plans to try to stab me this time to settle that old score."

"He didn't stab you," the woman shouted, and with the concern amping up on her face, she glanced behind her as the siren grew closer. When she whipped back toward Caroline, the fury had returned to her eyes. "So help me, you'd better not try to manipulate his feelings. You're a weak spot for Bodie, and I don't want you trying to brainwash him or something."

Caroline wanted to laugh. Jesus. What a piece of work. This Jordana idiot and the asshole Bodie deserved each other.

But she immediately rethought that.

She couldn't wish Bodie on her worst enemy, and while this woman was a delusional pain in the butt, she wasn't an enemy. In fact, she was someone to be pitied since it was possible Bodie would turn the knife on his bride if he got the chance.

"Oz, continue background info," Nash said, but this time the AI's response must have gone through his earbud because Caroline couldn't hear it.

A cruiser came tearing up the road toward her house. Not a county one but rather San Antonio PD, which was a good forty miles away.

"SAPD probably had a tail on her," Nash muttered to her. "Jordana's from San Antonio."

That made sense. There had to be an intense manhunt going on to find Bodie, and the cops would reason he might go to his wife. Apparently not though since Bodie had taken the exit toward her house. Of course, this could be some kind of ruse by Jordana to try to distract her so that Bodie could sneak up on her.

That sent Caroline firing glances all around her. And she silently cursed. It was already happening. This place she'd carved out for herself was starting to feel no longer safe, and she hated Bodie for that. Of course, she hated him for a lot of reasons, but that was one more to add to the list.

"I'm Detective Malley," a tall, blond-haired cop said as he bolted from the cruiser. He drew his gun. So did the female brunette in a uniform who came out from the passenger's side.

"They're legit," Nash explained, obviously getting some kind of info through his earpiece. "SAPD sent them out. Detective Jace Malley and Officer Amanda Gonzales."

"Is Bodie McKenna here?" Malley called out.

That was apparently the question of the day. "Not that I know of," Caroline settled for saying.

"You're Caroline Maverick?" Malley asked, and he seemed to do a mental doubletake when his attention landed on Nash. "And you're Nash McKenna from Maverick Ops."

It shouldn't have surprised her that Malley had immediately linked Nash's name with her mother's company. Maverick Ops often got a lot

20

of publicity. Mostly good press for the rescues and such they'd done.

"And you're Bodie's brother," Malley added to Nash. "Where is he?"

"No idea whatsoever," Nash replied. "But his wife seems to believe he'll be coming here."

"Not because Bodie still loves her," Jordana said lightning fast. "He loves me now. He married me."

Caroline went ahead and rolled her eyes and didn't hold back a very loud huff. "Insecure and gullible," she muttered.

"And rich," Nash supplied. Info he'd almost certainly gotten from Oz. "Her daddy is Leland Harris, owner of many, many businesses in central Texas. Jordana is his only child and lives off a trust fund."

Caroline had to wonder if Jordana had used some of her money to help Bodie escape. Maybe so husband and wife could ride off into the sunset and live happily ever after. If so, then it clearly hadn't turned out the way Jordana had wanted.

"Where's Bodie?" Malley demanded from Jordana.

Jordana opened her mouth, closed it, and again seemed to go through the rethinking process of what to say. "I don't know, but I wouldn't put it past her to have murdered him and hidden the body. You should look inside that big building. And her house."

"He's not inside the *big building*," Nash supplied. "I haven't searched the house yet."

"We'll do that," the female cop said. "We'll search the Mercedes, too, in case he's hiding in the trunk."

That shot some alarm through Caroline, and it twisted away at her that Bodie could still have that effect on her.

"Open the trunk," Malley told Jordana, and he looked up at Nash and Caroline. "We tailed her here so we know this vehicle is registered to her. It was also seen in the vicinity of the prison around the time that Bodie escaped."

"I was visiting my husband," the woman howled as she used the keypad to pop the trunk. "I had no idea he wasn't there."

"So, he didn't fill you in on his plans for the future?" Nash asked, and this time, he let the sarcasm reign.

Jordana's eyes narrowed again. "He wouldn't have wanted to involve me in something that could get me in trouble. And it probably wasn't his idea to escape. Something must have happened. Someone must have threatened his life, or mine, for this to have happened."

Caroline didn't get a chance to respond to that because she heard the whirring sound of a helicopter. She looked up, thinking that it might belong to SAPD, but then she spotted the logo on the tail.

Maverick Ops.

"Great," she grumbled. Her mother was here.

And Ruby was piloting the helicopter. Of

course, she was. She had done that plenty of times during her military career.

All conversation halted to an abrupt stop, mainly because it was impossible to be heard over the sound of the chopper, but Caroline noticed the noise didn't stop Nash from doing his whole protector thing. He still had his gun drawn, and he moved back in front of her.

Caroline kept watch, too, because, hey, she wasn't that clueless teenager.

From the corner of her eye, she saw her mother land the helicopter in her pasture and cursed at the wildflowers that were crushed. Ruby made a quick exit, heading straight toward them.

Her mother was wearing a dark gray business suit, but she still managed to look as if she had on a uniform—complete with her rank. Of course, she'd worn a uniform for so many years, twenty-three of them, that it was probably imprinted on her body or something.

Caroline tried, and failed, not to scowl about that.

"That's Ruby Maverick," Nash said when he saw the female cop shift to take aim in Ruby's direction.

"Yeah. It is. I recognize her from her pictures in the media. She's head of Maverick Ops, and Miss Caroline Maverick here is her daughter," Malley supplied, and he motioned for his fellow cop to stand down while he resumed his search of the trunk of the Mercedes.

"It's empty," Malley announced. "But I'll have the CSIs go over it and the interior in case she gave her husband a lift somewhere."

"I didn't," Jordana insisted.

"The CSIs will still go over it," Malley fired back, and he obviously wasn't any more pleased with the woman than Caroline and Nash were.

Malley turned when Ruby got closer and gave her a nodded greeting, along with a "Ma'am."

Ruby nodded a greeting in return, and with her gaze sweeping around the grounds, she continued toward Nash and her. Once she reached them, she lifted her hand just a fraction as if she might touch or hug Caroline.

She didn't though.

Must have remembered her military bearing, Caroline thought with all the rancor that went with pretty much any thought about her mother.

No PDA for Colonel Maverick.

In fact, not much parenting either. Or no big part in being a wife. That had culminated in her mother not even being near her husband's bedside when the aggressive form of cancer had claimed him.

Hence, the rancor on Caroline's part.

Her father had been her world. The best dad ever. And he should have had his wife by his side as he'd drawn his last breath. Instead, said wife had been thousands of miles away, saving the life of someone else. Someone she likely didn't even know.

"Thank you for getting here so fast," Ruby told Nash. Hearing her words caused Caroline's attention to shift back to her. "Has there been any sign of Bodie?"

"None." Nash tipped his head to Jordana. "But that's his wife, Jordana Harris McKenna."

Her mother dropped her usual poker face expression for a raised eyebrow. "I knew he'd married. I kept tabs on him," she tacked onto that when she glanced at Caroline. "Did his wife help him escape?"

"To be determined," Nash said, and he fired more glances around. "Look, it's probably best if Caroline stays back from the door, but I'd like to go inside and check the place with the cops."

"I'll wait here with her," Ruby was quick to say, and she eased back her jacket to put her hand over a gun in a shoulder holster.

"Great," Caroline muttered, but she didn't nix the idea.

Her house did indeed need to be checked, and while she was ready, willing, and able to take on Bodie, it would be stupid for her to turn down backup.

Even when backup was her mother.

Caroline stepped further back into her workshop with her mother taking over Nash's position when he headed into her house. The female cop stayed with Jordana, clearly standing guard.

"I'm getting some of the details of Bodie's

escape," her mother commented, tapping her earpiece. "I'm betting he had help, and his wife has the money to make it happen."

There were so many ways Caroline could take this conversation, but she went with the one that'd surprised her. "You kept tabs on Bodie?"

"Of course I did," her mother said in her no-nonsense way. "He tried to murder my daughter, so I wanted to make sure he...behaved himself in prison."

Caroline tried to wrap her mind around what that meant, and she silently cursed. "You thought he might try to arrange for someone to come after me?"

"I considered it," her mother confirmed. "And I took steps to make sure it didn't happen." She paused, said one single word of profanity. "I didn't take enough steps though to keep you safe, and I'm sorry about that."

That rift was still there, but that didn't mean Caroline wanted Ruby to beat herself up about something that was totally out of her control. Then again, maybe her mother believed she could indeed control everything.

"You sent Nash," Caroline reminded her. "He came in all *John Wick* and ready."

"He's Bodie's brother," her mother muttered after a long pause. "I didn't want you seeing him to trigger any memories for you."

Caroline shook her head. "I don't associate Nash with my memories of Bodie. I associate Nash with…"

Too bad she'd even added those last four words. And now her pause had caused her mother to glance back at her. In that glance, Ruby managed to study Caroline's face, and whatever she saw there had her muttering more profanity.

"Don't worry," Caroline said, not bothering to take the snark out of her voice. "Nash won't touch the boss' daughter even if I want him to."

Her mother would have almost certainly had a stinging comeback for that if Nash and Malley hadn't run out of her house. Caroline's heart dropped when she saw Nash's expression.

"What happened?" Caroline asked. "Did you find something in my house?"

"We haven't finished searching it yet. But a drone spotted someone matching Bodie's description," Nash spelled out, looking Caroline straight in the eyes. "If it's Bodie, he slipped into the woods. Those woods," he added.

And Nash pointed directly behind Caroline.

CHAPTER THREE

———— ☆ ————

Nash was already working out the logistics of how this search would play out, and he knew Ruby, the cops, and Caroline were no doubt doing the same thing.

Apparently, Jordana was, too.

"Bodie," the woman said on a sharp rise of breath, and she would have no doubt started sprinting toward those woods if Officer Gonzales hadn't stepped in front of her and held her back.

"Mrs. McKenna, you're not leaving," Detective Malley insisted, and he glanced around the woods.

Nash could see the debate that Malley was having with himself, so he threw out a suggestion. "You, Officer Gonzales, and my boss can stay here with Caroline, and I can—"

That was as far as Nash got before the objections started.

"I have to get to my husband now," Jordana insisted while she frantically shook her head. "You can't keep me here."

"I can and will keep you here," Malley fired back.

"And I want to go with you to look for the sonofabitch who tried to kill me," Caroline stated, spearing Nash with her fiery gaze. "It's not up for debate," she added when Ruby opened her mouth. "Think it through, Mom. Would I be safer here or with Nash, one of your highly trained operatives who stands the best chance of finding the piece of crap escapee?"

Ruby closed her mouth, and it seemed as if she was trying to rein in what would have been an order for Caroline to stay put and inside the workshop. An order her daughter likely wouldn't follow.

So, Nash spelled out the argument for Caroline.

"Bodie might not have a knife this time but rather a gun," he told Caroline. "He could want you in the woods so he can shoot you."

"Then, let's not give him what he wants," Caroline immediately countered. She tipped her head to his SUV. "Certainly you've got a Kevlar vest or two in there that'll protect us."

Nash silently did a whole bunch of cursing. "A vest won't stop you from dying from a head shot."

"And me being here won't prevent one either," Caroline was equally quick to point out. "In fact, Bodie could be out there waiting for the biggest threat to head off into those woods so he can charge in here after me. You're the biggest threat, Nash. Not them." She motioned to the cops. "Not my mother."

Despite Ruby's huff at being dismissed as that

biggest threat, Caroline had a point, damn it, but Nash didn't believe the cops were incompetent. They could stand on their own. Ruby could, too. But Bodie likely wouldn't see a fifty-something-year-old woman as a challenge.

She was.

But Bodie probably wouldn't realize it.

His brother was basically a chicken shit coward who had attacked a woman from behind. A woman half his size. So, yeah, the coward might indeed plan on waiting until his odds were better at getting to Caroline.

"Maybe Bodie isn't here for her," Jordana complained, her voice a nasally whine. "He could be coming here to get me. I'm his wife, and he loves me."

Everyone ignored her, and Nash turned to Ruby. Not for a whispered conversation though. He needed the cops to hear this, but most importantly, they needed to come up with a plan and act on it.

Fast.

Nash didn't want Bodie seeing them and tucking tail and running when he realized that Caroline wasn't alone and defenseless.

Though defenseless no longer applied to her, that's for sure.

Caroline seemed more than capable of protecting herself. Still, all the training and skillset in the world wouldn't prevent being killed from a lucky shot.

"I have at least three vests in the SUV," Nash pointed out.

That was apparently all that Ruby needed to know since she could easily see the determination on her daughter's face. Ruby nodded, giving him approval for the plan.

"Detective," Nash said, turning to Malley. "A county deputy should be here any minute. Are you okay with Ruby, Caroline, and me going after the suspect while you and Officer Gonzales remain with Mrs. McKenna?"

Nash had purposely used the *Mrs.* as a not so subtle reminder that a couple of things could happen. a) Bodie might indeed come for Jordana or b) Jordana might try to help her husband in some way. That could include attacking a cop or two to run into those woods after her asshole spouse.

"You don't have the authority to arrest Bodie," Malley reminded him, and for a moment Nash thought the detective was going to try to nix the plan. He didn't though. "So, if you find him, detain him and call me. As soon as the county deputy arrives, I'll join you on the search."

Malley rattled off his phone number, and Nash gave a verbal command to Oz to put it in his contacts. Then, Nash hurried toward his SUV to get those vests.

Part of him wanted to stop moving and just continue to think this through. But he knew he wouldn't be able to come up with anything that wouldn't involve Caroline being tucked away and out of harm. If she was with him, she could be a target, and the same could be said if she wasn't with him.

Praying this was the right thing to do, Nash came back with the three vests, and Caroline, Ruby, and he quickly got them on.

"Oz, is there an update from the drone?" Nash asked.

"No further sighting of the suspect," Oz supplied.

Nash took out his backup weapon and handed it to Caroline. "Best not to take a knife to a gun fight, huh?" she remarked, sheathing her knife.

"Something like that," Nash muttered. "Stay low and behind me. If things go wrong, get down. Repeat that last part to me."

She didn't huff, but it was close. "If things go wrong, get down. And what will you do?" Caroline tacked onto that.

"I'll neutralize the threat," he said.

He was aware that sounded cocky, but it was true. It was something he'd had a lot of experience doing first as an Air Force Combat Rescue Office and then working for Ruby. Normally though, he worked alone or with another trained operative who didn't happen to be his boss.

Or the attacker's target.

Both of those things were only going to add to the tension, and the stakes, of this search.

Hurrying to get them out of the open, Nash led the way toward the woods with Caroline behind him and Ruby at the rear. All were armed. All were ready.

Hopefully.

"Don't you dare hurt my husband," Jordana shouted.

He didn't know whose groan was the most intense. Ruby's, Caroline's or his. But hearing the woman's voice was a reminder that he needed to do a deeper dive on her so he could figure out if she had a part in what was happening now. Because everything she was saying and doing could be an act. A distraction to allow her husband to have another go at Caroline.

"Oz, continue drone surveillance," Nash instructed.

He needed that recon to detect anyone near them so he'd have a heads up, and they wouldn't get ambushed. Of course, it was possible Bodie had already spotted the drone and was staying out of sight and behind cover.

But to get to Caroline, he'd have to show himself.

Nash breathed just slightly easier when they finally made it out of the clearing and into the woods. Not merely a cluster of trees either. These were actual woods, choked with towering live oaks, cedars, and redbuds. They were thick enough to create a canopy that shut out enough of the sunlight to affect visibility.

They kept moving, stepping over dead leaves and sticks and dodging the underbrush that scratched against them as they passed. Behind him, he could hear Caroline's breathing. On the fast and heavy side. No surprise there. Despite wanting to dole out some payback, she had to be scared.

Ruby was probably feeling a whole bunch of that fear, too. Even though Caroline and she technically weren't close, this was still her child. A child in the potential path of a killer.

"Drone has detected someone," Oz said in his ear. "Approximately twenty feet ahead at your two o'clock."

Nash automatically shifted a little to the right. But he didn't see anyone. "Is the target moving?" Nash whispered.

"No," was Oz's reply.

So, Bodie was lying in wait. The coward's way.

"Stay crouched down," Nash whispered to Caroline.

He headed further to the right, hoping to come up on Bodie from the side. Of course, Bodie would almost certainly be able to hear them coming. Might be able to see them, too, but Nash didn't want to go at him head on, not with Caroline in the potential line of fire.

Caroline made a soft gasp that had his heart crashing against his ribs, and Nash whipped his head around to look at her. However, her attention was on the ground where he saw a copperhead slithering away.

Hell.

He'd been so caught in looking for the human piece of shit snake that he hadn't noticed the actual snake. Good thing it hadn't bitten one of them, and he continued walking, this time volleying some glances at the ground. At least if they encountered a rattlesnake, it'd give them some warning.

"Bodie?" someone called out.

That caused Nash, Caroline, and Ruby to freeze. Because it wasn't Jordana's voice. This was a man. And it wasn't someone's voice that Nash recognized.

"Bodie?" the guy repeated. "Hey, man. Is that you?"

Nash didn't answer. Instead, he got them moving again, closing in on the sound of their visitor.

Who the hell was this? Bodie's accomplice maybe? Or someone that Bodie had sent after Caroline? Either way, Nash was going to shut him down.

After trudging along another couple of minutes, Nash finally spotted the man. Definitely not Bodie. This guy was shorter, about five-ten, and he had fashionably messy dark blond hair pulled back in a ponytail. He had sort of a celebrity vibe about him, what with his stubble and clothes. Black jeans and olive green tee that looked tailored made.

And no visible weapon.

That didn't mean he wasn't armed though.

Nash was only about ten feet away from the guy when he must have heard the approaching footsteps. He pivoted in that direction. Instant alarm shot over his face, and he reached in the back waist of his pants. No doubt to draw a weapon.

"Don't," Nash immediately warned him. "Put your hands in the air so I can see them."

The guy didn't comply right away, not until he'd given all three of them a long look. He must have realized he was seriously outnumbered and outgunned because his hands went up.

"You're Bodie's brother?" the man asked.

Nash ignored his question and went with one of his own. It would be the first of many things he wanted to know. "Who the hell are you?"

"Eddie," he said, his voice cracking a little. "Eddie Mulcrone. Is Bodie with you?" But then, he immediately shook his head. "No, Bodie wouldn't be with any of you lot. I know who you are," he spat out, tipping his head to Caroline and Ruby. "Did you kill him? Did you bastards kill Bodie?'

There was a lot of info in that handful of remarks. Something key was missing though. "How do know Bodie?"

Despite it being an obvious question to Nash, apparently this Eddie hadn't seen it coming because he looked somewhat nonplussed. "We did time together, but I got out last year. Bodie's like a brother to me," he tacked onto that. "Not like you. You turned your back on him. I didn't."

"Great," Nash muttered. "Another fan of a chicken shit felon. I'm guessing that means you also know his wife?"

Eddie's mouth tightened. "Yeah, I know Jordana. Can't say I like her much, but since Bodie married her and all, I tolerate her."

That was more than Nash could do. He had no intentions of tolerating his sister-in-law.

"Why are you out in these woods?" Nash asked, and then he added the most important question of all. "Were you here to try to kill Caroline?"

"No," Eddie was quick to say. "I was here to leave something for Bodie…" He stopped and must have realized he was about to admit to a crime. "I, uh, was going to convince him to turn himself in."

"Sure you were," Nash remarked, and Caroline and Ruby gave similar responses. "Is Bodie supposed to meet you here?"

Eddie shook his head. Too fast. Too firm of a response. "No. I was supposed to leave him this." He lowered his hand toward his pocket, but Nash stopped him by moving into a shooting stance. "Don't get all trigger happy. It's just a phone and some money, that's all."

"So, aiding and abetting an escaped felon," Nash concluded.

"No," Eddie practically shouted. "It's not like that. Yeah, I brought the stuff, but I was going to hang around and wait for Bodie to show up. Then, I was going to convince him to turn himself in." He shifted his narrowed eyes to Caroline. "I was going

37

to make him understand that she and her mother will try to kill him and cover it up."

Nash wondered how Bodie had managed to brainwash this dipshit and Jordana. Then again, Bodie had always been the charmer. On the surface anyway. And he'd likely used that charm eighteen years ago to convince Caroline to go out with him. But the charm was just a veneer, and beneath, he was twisted and dangerous.

"Ruby, could you text Detective Malley and let him know we're about to escort Eddie to him so the two of them can have a chat," Nash said.

Eddie cursed a blue streak. "You're taking me to the fuckin' cops? Why? I didn't do anything wrong."

"Put your hands on top of your head," Nash ordered, and knowing that Ruby and Caroline would cover him, he went to frisk the man. No gun. But a knife that Nash confiscated and slid into his own pocket. "Move."

Eddie continued to curse and complain, but he started walking, probably because Nash gave him a shove in the back. Nash and the others followed him, and Nash continued to keep watch just in case Bodie was indeed around. But if he was, the drone hadn't picked up on it, or Oz would have alerted him.

"Don't know why I have to talk to the fuckin' cops," Eddie went on, kicking at a clump of twigs and leaves with far more force than necessary. "They should be talking to Jordana's daddy. I'm bettin' he's the one who set all of this shit up."

"What shit?" Nash asked.

"Setting up Bodie to escape, that's what," Eddie snapped. "Let me tell you, that wasn't Bodie's idea. Why escape when he'd be getting parole next go around? He would have been out in maybe less than a year."

Nash heard Caroline's quick intake of breath. Yeah, it was a chilling thought that his brother might have gotten parole, but Nash had figured it probably would have happened eventually. Bodie had already served eighteen years of a twenty-five-year sentence. Normally, the max would have been twenty, but there'd been some illegal weapons and resisting arrest charges tacked onto that.

"So, what does Leland Harris have to do with Bodie escaping?" Nash pressed.

"Shit. Everything, man. I figure Daddy Rich Ass set it all up so that Bodie didn't have a choice but to escape. Maybe because somebody inside was going to murder him if he didn't get the hell out of there."

Caroline huffed. "And why would Mr. Harris do that?"

Eddie made a duh sound. "So that Bodie would be killed. No way in fuckin' hell does Daddy Rich Ass want his pretty little princess daughter married to the likes of Bodie. This way, he gets rid of Bodie without getting his hands dirty, and his idiot daughter won't hate him for doing her husband in."

Well, if Leland Harris had indeed set this up,

then his hands were indeed dirty. But that notion sounded like a long shot to Nash. Still, it was possible. A father could do all sorts of things to protect his child.

"You ought to be careful about Leland Harris," Eddie went on and glanced back at Caroline. "I figure he's planning to kill you and set up Bodie to take the blame. That way, if the cops or y'all don't murder Bodie, then he'll go back inside on death row. A win-win for Daddy Rich Ass."

Nash wished that theory didn't tighten his gut. But it did. And it was something that would need to be investigated.

They reached the clearing, and Nash spotted the county cruiser now in Caroline's drive. He also saw Malley lifting his phone before using it to make a call. Nash's own phone rang, and he answered it on speaker.

"No sign of Bodie?" Malley asked, but it was obvious from his urgent tone that he had something else to say.

"None, but maybe our guest will be able to tell us where he is. Is something wrong?" Nash went ahead and asked.

"Yeah," Malley verified. "After the deputy got here, I went inside the house to finish looking around." He paused. "And I found something."

CHAPTER FOUR

———— ☆ ————

Caroline had no idea what had put that doom and gloom look on Detective O'Malley's face, but it was obvious that he needed to tell her something bad.

Or rather show her.

Malley was on her porch and motioned for Nash, Ruby, and her to come into the house as soon as Nash handed off Eddie to Officer Gonzales.

"Is Bodie inside?" Caroline came out and asked.

Malley shook his head but didn't add more. He just led them through her living room and into the hall to the bedrooms.

With each step she took, Caroline's heartbeat kicked up even faster, and her grip tightened on the gun that Nash had given her. If Bodie was indeed here though, Malley must not have believed his own gun would be needed since he currently had it holstered.

So, maybe Bodie was dead.

That would mesh with what Eddie had said about Jordana's father, Leland, wanting Bodie out of the way. Had Leland killed Bodie with the plan to make it look as if she'd done it?

She hadn't.

But if thoughts could kill, Bodie would have already been roasting in the lowest level of hell.

Malley stopped outside her bedroom door, and stepping to the side, he drew in a long breath. "Obviously, don't touch anything. The CSIs are on the way and will process the scene."

The *scene*. As in a crime.

Since her imagination was going full throttle, Caroline steeled herself up and went to the door. And she froze. Just froze.

Not a body.

But blood. So much blood. It covered her bed, turning the soft blue quilt crimson red. In the center was a knife that had been stabbed into the mattress.

Then, there were the photos.

Dozens of them were scattered on the floor. Photos of her. Some recent. Some from back then, when she'd been eighteen. Most of the images had been taken from long range.

Except for one.

It had been propped up on her headboard and was much larger than the others. Bodie's face stared back at her. Not an old photo either. This one had to have been a recent one since he had a few wrinkles at the corners of his eyes. And in the picture, he was grinning and sporting a triumphant look.

"Hell," Nash muttered.

That's when she realized he was right next to

her and had taken hold of her arm. Ruby was behind her, and her mother's breath wasn't as steady as usual.

"I'm guessing these weren't your photos?" Malley asked.

Caroline shook her head. "No. I've never seen them before. That's not my knife either."

It was one she recognized though. Or rather she recognized the handle that had been made from a stag antler. She knew because it was identical to the one Bodie had used on her.

"It'll be a skinning knife," she muttered. "With a hook at the tip."

Just saying that robbed Caroline of her breath, and she felt that razor-sharp hooked blade slice into her. Felt it over and over again. Then, the images came.

The blur of frenetic motion.

The pain.

The godawful pain.

"Steady," Nash murmured, and he moved in front of her, cupping her chin and forcing eye contact. "Steady," he repeated, his voice calm enough, but even though she was on the verge of a serious panic attack, Caroline could see this had gotten to him, too.

"Whose blood is that?" She managed barely a whisper and silently cursed her reaction. She didn't want to feel weak. She didn't want to feel scared.

But she did.

God help her, she did.

Caroline used Nash as an anchor. Or more of a lifeline. She locked gazes with his and picked up the rhythm of his breathing since it was a whole lot more level than hers was.

"It's probably fake," he said. "The color is off for it to be real." Nash paused, kept his focus solely on her. Kept his hand gripped on her shoulders. "Here's what I want you to do. Don't look at the bed or the pictures, but glance around the room and tell me if anything's missing. Can you do that?"

She nodded even though Caroline wasn't sure she could actually do as he'd asked. Still, she didn't resist when Nash eased to the side so she could have that look.

It was impossible not to notice all the blood, but she reminded herself that it was probably fake. The entire scene had been staged to terrify her. And it'd worked. Damn it, it'd worked, and that had to stop.

Caroline took in the rest of the room. The nightstand with her blown glass lamp that she'd made. Her phone charger and her tablet. There were a pair of panties and a bra tossed on the chair in the corner. Not part of the staging. She'd left them there when she'd gotten dressed that morning.

"Nothing's missing," she said.

"Good," Malley piped in. "Nothing else in the house seems to be out of place, but the back door appears to have been jimmied."

While Malley was talking, Nash led her away from the bedroom and back into the kitchen. He didn't have her sit, probably because this area would need to be checked by the CSIs as well.

"When would the intruder have gotten in?" Malley asked.

Caroline had to force herself to focus. "Anytime in the past six hours. That's when I went to blow glass in the workshop." She motioned toward the building that was visible from the window.

"Did you lock the house and turn on a security system when you left?" Malley pressed.

She had to mentally go through her morning routine. "Yes to the lock. No to the system. I also locked my workshop door once I was in there. I do that because I don't want anyone walking in and letting out the heat."

As she heard her own words, Caroline wanted to kick herself. Hard. All that self-defense training, and she hadn't taken the simple precaution of activating a security system, something she had for both buildings. Then again, she hadn't known Bodie was going to escape from prison, sneak into her house, and leave a bloody scene for her to find.

If it was Bodie, that is.

"Maybe Eddie did this," Caroline muttered.

"Or Jordana," Nash supplied.

Caroline made a quick sound of agreement. Jordana was a definite possibility since she obviously knew the address of the place. Added to that, the woman could have been carrying out

Bodie's orders.

Her mother dived into the conversation. "But whoever did this had to have access to those photos. At least three that I saw were of you in your dorm room eighteen years ago. They'd been taken from the window. Nighttime shots." She looked at Nash. "Was your brother into doing something like that?"

Because Nash's arm was right next to hers, Caroline felt his muscles tense. That must have felt like a kick to the teeth for her mother to throw out that "your brother." And to phrase it as if Nash had that genuine sibling connection that would allow him to be aware of such things.

"I'm not sure," Nash said. "I hadn't seen Bodie in years before he attacked Caroline." He paused. "But I've read the police reports and know that he stalked her, so I'm guessing he could have taken the photos then. Maybe he'd had them stored all this time and accessed them after he escaped."

The sound of an approaching vehicle stopped him from adding more, and Malley went to the front window to look out. "It's the CSIs. Caroline, do you have any clothes, meds or such you can pack that aren't in your bedroom? You shouldn't be here when the CSIs are going through the place."

"I'm sure there's stuff in the laundry room and the kitchen cabinets," she muttered.

"Good. Go ahead and pack some stuff, and we can work out where you can go," Malley added. "If you need something from your bedroom, I can have one of the CSIs get it after they've recorded it."

"You can stay with me," her mother was quick to volunteer.

Caroline was equally quick to shake her head, and she looked at Nash. "Can I go to your place?"

She knew that put him in a difficult situation, but at that moment, she couldn't think of another alternative. She definitely didn't want to go to a hotel. Or to her mother's. Just being around Ruby could cause other memories to resurface. Really, crappy ones of her father's death, and Caroline couldn't deal with that and stay level about Bodie's antics.

"Of course, you can stay with me," Nash agreed, and Caroline didn't think it was her imagination that he'd dodged her mother's gaze when he said that.

"All right then. Let's get that stuff from the laundry room and kitchen. Then, I can have the CSIs get my phone charger and tablets," Caroline said, heading toward the laundry room.

With Nash right behind her.

She was thankful for it, too. At the moment, her house no longer seemed safe, and she'd take a heavily muscled, trained ops guy as her backup. She was also thankful that Ruby didn't tag along because she needed a moment to catch her breath. Easier to do that without her mother.

"I'm sorry," Nash muttered when they reached the laundry room. "If I could stomp Bodie's ass in the ground for you, I would."

That comment performed somewhat of a miracle because it made her smile. Well, her mouth went through the motions of one anyway. No real merriment made it to any other part of her body.

"If I could kick my mother's ass for you, I would," she countered as she opened the dryer and found the clothes that'd been there heaven knew how long. "That *your brother* remark. She could have at least just used the asshole's name and not connected him to you."

"But I am connected to him," Nash pointed out after a long sigh. "I'm connected to the asshole."

Caroline turned and gave him a flat look. "Only through random bits of DNA. Nothing more. I don't consider him your brother," she tacked onto that, remembering what her mother had said.

Recalling it caused her to huff, and she grabbed a handful of the clothes as if she'd declared war on them. "My mother was worried that me seeing you would remind me of the asshole. It doesn't." She threw the items into the laundry basket that she would use as a makeshift suitcase since her actual suitcase was in her closet. "It doesn't," she repeated when she didn't think she'd convinced Nash.

So, she tried to convince him another way.

A bad one.

Caroline leaned in and kissed him. She had a WTF moment, followed by something else. Something hot that packed a serious punch.

Nash made a sound, part grunt, part groan, but she was absolutely certain that he felt the punch, too. He took hold of her forearm, easing her closer. Pressing his mouth even harder against her.

Before he stepped back.

Because the kiss had created a mighty haze in her head, it took her a moment to realize they were no longer alone. Her mother was in the doorway.

Shit.

"Don't you dare give him the third degree about that," Caroline warned her mother. "I'm the one who kissed him."

"Yes, I saw that," Ruby commented, and she couldn't have had more disapproval if she'd tried in her voice and expression. She cleared her throat. "I, uh, wanted to let you know that you have a visitor. My gut tells me this isn't a good time for you to talk to him, but I didn't want to speak for you. For either of you," she added, shifting her attention to Nash.

"Who's the visitor?" Nash asked.

"Jordana's father, Leland Harris, and he wants to talk to the two of you," Ruby answered. "He claims he knows how to find Bodie."

CHAPTER FIVE

———— ☆ ————

Hell.

Nash didn't like people just showing up at Caroline's place. Not when one of those people was Leland Harris. They'd already had surprise "visits" from Jordana and Eddie, and apparently, they were about to add one more to the list.

"If you want to talk to him," Ruby continued, "then Detective Malley says it can't happen here inside the house."

Yeah, Nash had already come to that conclusion. Having Leland inside could screw with potential trace evidence.

Fibers and prints.

Maybe even some DNA.

Because if any of those things were found, Leland could argue they'd been left during his chat with Caroline and not when he'd been breaking in to leave that bloody mess in the bedroom.

That said, Nash figured if Leland was indeed behind that, if the man wanted to spur Caroline to kill Bodie, then he would have hired a minion to do it. Why get his rich hands dirty when he could just pay someone? Still, it was an unnecessary risk to bring him inside the house.

"We can use Caroline's studio," Nash suggested. That way, she wouldn't be out in the open, and since the place didn't have windows, a sniper wouldn't be able to target her there.

Ruby turned toward Caroline, no doubt to see if her daughter had any objections to that. Apparently, she didn't because she nodded, and on a heavy sigh, she started toward the front door.

Nash was right there with her and was glad she was still wearing the vest. That didn't mean though that he wanted her out in the open any longer than necessary. Once they reached the porch, Nash stepped in front of Caroline, and he did a sweeping glance around at the, well, chaos.

In addition to Caroline's, Jordana's, and his vehicles, there was the SAPD cruiser, the county cruiser, a CSI van, and a black limo that had to belong to Leland. Two CSIs were standing by the side of the van and were talking to Malley.

Jordana was by her car and was with a tall gray-haired man who had to be her father. They appeared to be arguing while a beefy guy wearing a black suit stood at a discrete distance. Probably a chauffeur or bodyguard.

Possibly Leland's minion.

Eddie was still there, too, and he was ranting about his rights to Officer Gonzales, who was mainly ignoring him and talking to someone on her radio that she had clipped to the shoulder lapel of her uniform.

Nash didn't linger in the chaos. He got Caroline moving, and he didn't breathe easier until they were in the workshop. With Ruby. Which, of course, stalled his whole breathing easier attempts. Still, he couldn't fault Ruby for wanting to be there and hear what Leland had to say.

When Malley spotted Nash and Caroline though, he stepped away and started toward them. "I'm guessing you'll be talking to Leland Harris in here?" the detective asked.

"Evidently," Caroline said. "I haven't gotten my things from the house yet though."

Malley whipped out a small notepad from his pocket and handed it and a pen to her. "If you could jot down what you need, I'll have the CSIs gather it up for you. Try to get enough for at least two days since I'm not sure how long it will take them to process the scene."

Nash figured it could turn out to be longer than two days. Not because the CSIs would need more time but because he didn't want Caroline returning here until Bodie was either back behind bars or dead. Nash was hoping Caroline would agree with him on that.

Hoping, too, that this close-quarters arrangement didn't turn into something else.

He was doing a whole lot of silent cursing about that kiss. And not because his boss had witnessed it either. The cursing was because it sure as hell should have never happened. There was this blasted heat between Caroline and him, but that heat was going to have to cool its ass down. That kind of entanglement could lead to a loss of focus, which in turn could get Caroline killed the hard way.

At Bodie's hand.

No way could Nash risk that happening again.

Caroline wrote down some things and handed the notepad back to Malley, who then in turn jogged back to the CSIs to give it to them. Malley didn't speak to them for long but instead turned and motioned for Leland to follow him to the workshop. Leland did.

And so did the minion.

"Have they been searched for weapons?" Nash asked Malley. Best to get that out of the way before asking Leland where Bodie was.

But it wasn't Malley who answered. It was Leland. "Yes, and trust me, my lawyer will have something to say about that."

"Trust me," Malley fired back, "my lieutenant would have something to say about that if I didn't follow standard protocols. Someone helped Bodie escape, and all indications are he'll come after Caroline. I'd be derelict in my duties if I didn't put her safety first."

Nash wanted to applaud the detective. Leland's scowl conveyed he didn't feel the same way.

"Both came here armed," Malley went on. "And, yes, they had the permits to carry. Their weapons are in my cruiser. They'll get them back as they're leaving." He hiked his thumb toward the beefy man. "FYI, this is Mr. Harris' driver and personal assistant. Roger Grange"

AKA minion.

"Mr. Harris, this is Caroline and Ruby Maverick and Nash McKenna, a security operative at Maverick Ops."

Leland spared Nash a glance and had moved on to nodding a greeting at Ruby when his attention flew back to Nash. "McKenna?"

Nash nodded. "Brother of the escaped convict," he readily provided.

Leland huffed and looked at Malley as if he might object to Nash's presence, but then he must have figured it wasn't an argument worth launching. Malley's raised eyebrow and *don't test me* expression probably played into that.

"I'm guessing since you work for Maverick Ops, you've been vetted," Leland muttered before he turned to Caroline. "I think you and I want the same thing. Bodie McKenna dead. Am I right?"

Caroline shrugged. "I'd settle for him going back to jail. With the new charges from the escape and attack on the nurse, he won't be getting out any time soon."

"He'd be better off dead," Leland snapped, and he glanced at his daughter through the open door.

Jordana was glaring at them. Maybe because she hadn't been invited to this discussion, or she might just know her dad was hellbent on giving her husband a civilian's version of a death sentence.

"Where's Bodie?" Nash came out and asked.

"Near here. I don't know his exact location," Leland tacked onto that, causing Caroline, Nash, and Malley to groan. "But every indication is that he'll try to get to Caroline."

Malley added a second huff. "You didn't have to drive all the way out here to tell us that. Do you or don't you know Bodie's whereabouts?"

Leland's scowl deepened. "Again, not specifically, but I have an entire team of private investigators on this. They're searching for him and will find him."

"Cops are looking for him, too," Nash pointed out. "So is Maverick Ops. What makes you think your team would be better at finding him?"

"Because I have a plan." Leland fixed his attention on Caroline. "If you're willing to be bait, we can draw Bodie out."

That brought on a bunch of cursing, some of it from Nash, Malley, and Ruby. Plenty more of it came from Caroline.

"I'm already bait," she snapped. "Wherever I am, wherever I go, that will be Bodie's destination."

Ruby took up the argument. "What do you expect her to do? Stand out in the pasture, arms open wide and with a target on her forehead? Well, it's not going to happen. It's not," she repeated with far more emotion than she usually showed. "Why don't you use your own damn daughter as bait? Certainly Bodie will want to see his *wife*?"

Leland's jaw muscles went to war with each other. "Wife in name only," he snarled. "I intend to fix that as soon as I talk some sense into Jordana."

So, he didn't approve of the marriage. No surprise there.

"Jordana seems to think she's in love with Bodie," Nash pointed out.

That didn't ease those tight jaw muscles. "Like I said, I intend to fix that. Once Bodie is out of the picture, then Jordana can do a reset and get her life back on track. And trust me, her track isn't anywhere near your sonofabitch brother."

Leland maybe thought that was an insult. It wasn't. In fact, Nash thought sonofabitch was a mild term for Bodie. He could think of much, much worse things to call him.

"So, you don't want to use Jordana as bait," Malley spelled out. "But you want to use Caroline. In theory, how would that work? I'm guessing it'd be more than standing in the open field?"

Leland seemed to be making a visible effort to corral his composure. "Caroline should put out the word that she wants to meet Bodie. She could do that through Bodie's lowlife friend, Eddie. Then, we could secure the meeting place and take Bodie down when he tries to kill Caroline."

"No," Nash was quick to say.

Ruby and Malley echoed the same.

Caroline laughed. Actually laughed.

"First of all, Bodie will know that's a trap. He doesn't want to meet with me," Caroline emphasized. "He wants to put the blade of a very sharp skinning knife, maybe a bullet, into me. And despite being a vicious would-be killer, he's not stupid. He won't come at me head-on, especially not in a situation he can't completely control. He'll want the surprise element. Or a situation where he has complete control. Then and only then, will he try to kill me."

And there it was. All laid out on that proverbial silver platter, and hearing it twisted a hard knot in Nash's gut. Because that was exactly what Bodie would try to do.

Nash had to make sure Bodie didn't get the chance.

"So, you're turning down my plan?" Leland asked through clenched teeth. Apparently, he wasn't accustomed to people telling him no.

"You don't have a plan," Nash pointed out. "You have a desire to eliminate your son-in-law."

Yeah, that last part was a dig to get back at him for the brother remark. And it hit paydirt.

"Fuck this," Leland snarled, and he walked out with the minion trailing along behind him.

Leland only made it a step outside the studio though when all hell broke loose.

CHAPTER SIX

———— ☆ ————

Caroline heard the hissing and crackling sound. Sounds that amplified within seconds, followed by an intense burst of heat. She could feel it even while in the doorway of the workshop.

"Something's on fire," she managed to say.

Just as she got a look of the *something*. Her house. Or rather what was left of it. At the moment, it was a giant fireball with ashes and flames raining down on her driveway.

"Oh, God," she blurted.

Her first instinct was to run toward the house, to try to save it, even though she knew it was well past that point. It was gone. In flames. Everything inside and the house itself were blazing.

There were shouts and curses as the people in the driveway scattered to get out of the way. She saw Jordana running toward the road. Eddie, too, with Officer Gonzales and the county deputy in pursuit.

She spotted Malley as well, not going after Eddie or Jordana but rather helping one CSI pull another away from the fire. Caroline thought the female CSI that they were dragging was unconscious. Hopefully not dead. But if she'd been inside the house, she certainly would be.

"Bodie," Caroline muttered.

"Maybe," Nash said, stepping in front of her again. Using his body as a human shield. He looked back at her. "There could be an incendiary device somewhere around the perimeter of the workshop."

Sweet heaven. She hadn't even considered that. But she was considering it now, and it gave her a hard punch of panic and adrenaline.

"We need to get to my SUV," Nash said after firing glances all around. "It's bullet resistant, and it's closer than the two cruisers."

It was, but there was still a good ten yards of space between the SUV and them. And the route was littered with burning debris. It'd be like running through a fiery obstacle course. Still, there weren't a lot of options here. Bodie, or whoever had set fire to her house, probably wouldn't have gotten the chance to plan an IED or some device on Nash's SUV.

She hoped.

"Stay between Ruby and me," Nash instructed.

That was all he said before he got them moving. Fast. He darted outside into the nightmare, weaving and dodging both the ground obstructions along with the ash and thick black smoke that was already billowing toward them. They were still a few feet away.

When their luck ran out.

Caroline heard the sound. And instantly knew what it was.

Gunfire.

Not a single shot, either. This was a barrage of bullets that slammed into the ground around them.

Her mother made a sharp gasping sound, and Caroline risked glancing behind her. Not hit. But rather shot in the Kevlar vest. It must have hurt, bad, because Ruby's face was sheathed with pain. That didn't stop her from moving though. She closed in, covering Caroline from behind.

The moment they reached the front end of the SUV, Nash pushed Caroline to the side of it. That's when she realized the shots were coming from the woods. A sniper maybe. So, the SUV could offer some protection from bullets.

But not from the fire.

A sudden gust of wind caused the blaze and sparks to fly. Hot little embers sailed out at them, and Caroline had to duck all the way down and cover her head.

"Get in the SUV," Nash told her. "And lay all the way down on the seat. The glass can resist bullets, but some might get through. Ruby, you get in, too."

Ruby immediately shook her head. "I'll be all right," she insisted, convincing absolutely no one that it was true. She was still grimacing and sucking in some hard breaths.

And she was on fire.

Caroline cursed when she saw one of the embers land in Ruby's hair. It flamed up, and Caroline did the first thing that came to mind. She grabbed a handful of dirt from the nearby flower bed and used it to extinguish the fire.

"In the SUV," Nash repeated, and this time it sounded like an order.

Caroline listened, mainly because she didn't want Nash distracted by her not doing as he'd said. Added to that, the embers were still landing, stinging her exposed skin. They were likely doing the same to Nash as well, but he stayed put, partly behind the cover of the SUV, while he scanned the woods for the shooter.

Ruby tapped her earpiece and requested help from the drone. Good. Maybe the drone could pinpoint who was doing this.

Was it Bodie?

Maybe.

Or maybe someone he'd convinced to create this kind of carnage. In fact, the carnage could be a ruse all so she could be shot.

But she immediately rethought that.

Bodie would want to do the kill himself. He wouldn't want to hand that "pleasure" to someone else.

The shots continued, slamming into the SUV and one skipped off the roof just as Caroline got the door open. She dived inside and moved to the passenger's seat to give Ruby and maybe even Nash some room to get in.

They didn't.

Damn it. They didn't.

They stayed there, shoulder to shoulder, ducking bullets and looking for their attacker.

During her training, Caroline had learned a lot about firearms, and she was pretty sure the handguns they had didn't have the range to return fire. Since Nash had had three Kevlar vests in the SUV, it was likely he had other things. Things that could help put an end to this. She climbed over the console that divided the front seats and checked the back.

And she found a stash of guns and equipment.

She pulled out a rifle with a scope and scrambled back to the driver's side door to stick it out for Nash.

"Thanks," he muttered. "There's a second one. Get it for Ruby."

Caroline did, handing it off to him so he could in turn pass it to Ruby. "By the way, I'm a good shot," Caroline let him know. "A very good shot," she emphasized.

"Then, get a third one for yourself but still stay down."

She did, after she sighed, and Caroline was about to ask if they needed ammo, but she saw Nash lift the rifle and use the scope to take aim.

"Drone feed in," Ruby said. "One shooter. A male dressed all in black and wearing a balaclava. Armed with a sniper rifle. He's in the cluster of live oaks. There." She pointed to the same area where

Nash already had the rifle pointed.

It wasn't close. She'd done plenty of target training, and she hadn't lied when she'd told Nash that she was a good marksman, but this distance would have been a serious challenge for her. Of course, it was possibly a challenge for the shooter, too, since he hadn't actually hit them.

Not yet anyway.

And coming in closer toward them probably would have been akin to a suicide mission what with three cops, Nash, and Ruby on the scene.

"Stay down, everyone," Nash shouted.

And he fired.

Since he was so close to her, the thick blasts from the shotgun thundered in her ears, and the shots just kept on coming. She counted to five before she heard something else.

Ruby cursed, and she pressed her fingers to her earpiece where she was no doubt getting bad news.

"The shooter dropped down out of the tree," her mother blurted. "The sonofabitch is getting away."

CHAPTER SEVEN

———— ☆ ————

"No," Caroline shouted.

Nash whirled toward her, a horrible thought flying through his mind.

That she'd been hit. That one of the gunman's bullets had made it through the SUV and into her.

But she hadn't been hit.

And he saw the reason for her shout. The anger and frustration were in every part of her expression. All of those emotions must have just come pouring out of her, and she'd released it in that ear-piecing yell.

Like Nash, Caroline didn't want Bodie, or whoever the hell this was, getting away. Nash wanted him stopped and taken into custody. He wanted him to pay for ripping Caroline's life apart at the seams.

"I'm calling for more backup," the county deputy yelled. "Nobody go in pursuit. I'll get a team out here."

Nash wouldn't hold out hope that the team would get there in time, especially since the shooter probably had a vehicle stashed nearby and was at the moment already in it and heading to heaven knew where.

Or he could be waiting to gun down anyone who went into the clearing.

Either way, Nash wasn't going after him, but instead he instructed the person monitoring the drone to keep track of the shooter. If they could see where he was going, they could catch him.

Well, they could do that after Caroline was safe, that is. And all right. It was obvious at the moment that she wasn't anywhere in that realm of being *all right*.

"No," she repeated, but this time it came out more like a sob. "I won't cry. I. Will. Not. Cry."

But tears watered her eyes. Tears that crushed his heart, and once again, he wished he could make the asshole pay for putting her through this.

"Go ahead and get her out of here before the fire department jams up the driveway," Ruby whispered to him. "Slade is only a couple of miles out and will be here soon to follow you for backup."

Slade. His other brother. And not an asshole killer. Slade was former special ops and one of the best operatives Ruby had. Nash couldn't think of anyone else he'd rather have back him up unless it was his baby brother, Jericho. Yet another operative.

Being a hero ran in the family.

Then again, so did killing.

That was especially true since their father

had almost certainly murdered their mother and gotten away with it. Clearly, Bodie had followed in their dear old dad's footsteps.

"Once you have Caroline safe at your place," Ruby went on, "Slade can come back here and join the search for Bodie and the shooter if that turns out to be someone else. Sorry to pull your brother away from you after you're home, but Slade's one of my best trackers."

He was indeed. "I want Slade on the hunt," Nash let her know.

"Good." Ruby gathered her breath and rubbed the spot where the bullet had hit the Kevlar. "I'm fine," she insisted, obviously seeing what he'd noticed. "I'll stay behind and do clean up," she tacked onto that.

Normally, he wouldn't have taken her up on an offer like that. Because clean-up was going to be a bear. But Caroline had been through enough, and they could get to his place and regroup.

He got in the SUV, putting the rifle back in the case, and he looked at Caroline. "We're going to my house about twenty miles from here," he said. "With Slade following us on the way there. Are you okay with that?"

He wanted to give her a say in this, but the alternative was to go to a safe house. His place was just as safe as any that Ruby could set up for them. And they wouldn't have to wait for that set up either.

Caroline nodded. "I need to get away from

here," she muttered.

"Understood." And her mother had obviously understood it as well.

It wasn't easy, what with the debris covering the driveway, but Nash was able to maneuver his SUV around the other vehicles and responders by driving through Caroline's flower beds. Yet another kind of destruction to something she'd obviously tended and taken care of. Then again, with the house gone, it was possible she wouldn't even be coming back here.

"I don't have any clothes," she said, maybe latching onto that less serious problem than everything else they were facing.

"Oz, arrange for some clothes, underwear, and toiletries to be brought to my house for Caroline. Arrange for the usual food delivery, too. I just got back from an op," he added to Caroline, "and I haven't had time to do groceries."

Again, that was one of those less serious problems, but he would eventually want her to eat something.

He drove just a few feet away from the others and then stopped, waiting for Slade. They didn't have to wait long before he spotted Slade's familiar black van. His brother obviously spotted them, too, and pulled to the side of the road so that Nash could get ahead of him. Nash didn't waste any time driving away.

And keeping watch.

After all, they had to drive right past those

woods where the shooter had been, and it was possible the dickhead was still there, waiting for another chance to fire some bullets. Nash doubted it though. Soon, there'd be cops and investigators scouring those woods, and the shooter, or Bodie, wouldn't want to be within miles of the place.

But where would Bodie go?

If his goal was to get to Caroline, and Nash was certain that it was, then Bodie could possibly be looking for her. At Nash's place. Maybe Ruby's, too. However, it wouldn't be easy to set fires and stage a bloody scene at either of those two locations because of the security. Bodie would be aware of that, too. He would have heard of Maverick Ops' reputation with such things.

So, Bodie would have to lure out Caroline or send in someone who could get close enough to her to do the luring. Again, not an easy task since Caroline and he would be on heightened alert.

They drove in silence for a while, passing by all that beautiful scenery he'd passed on the mad rush to get to her. This time though, Nash had a new task. To keep watch for any signs of another attack. Thankfully, he didn't see anything out of the ordinary so he kept threading through the backroads toward his house.

"Sorry about that outburst back there," Caroline muttered, yanking his attention back to her. "And these," she said, wiping away some tears. "I'm not a boo-hooer, and I'm not about to start now."

"I think you had a valid reason for a few tears," he pointed out.

The sound she made let him know she didn't agree with that. "I thought I was done with tears," she added, her voice barely louder than a whisper. "I did enough of that after the attack."

Yeah, he was betting she had. A long, painful recovery, and even though Bodie had been in jail throughout it, that didn't mean Caroline wouldn't have been looking in every corner and in every shadow for a killer.

He hated that.

Hated Bodie a billion times over for putting her through a nightmare cycle that would never end. Never. Because even if Bodie was dead and buried, that wouldn't erase the memories of the attack that had nearly left her dead.

"Part of me does want to stand out in the open and shout for Bodie to come after me," she added a moment later. "That final showdown where I turn the tables on him and kick his ass." Caroline paused. "But another part of me is worried I might freeze, that I might slingshot back to him stabbing me. I certainly didn't do much fighting back that time."

"I'm sorry," he said because he didn't know what else to say. "If I could undo all of that, I would."

"Same," she was quick to say. "FYI, I never actually dated him. I want you to know that. I had coffee with him at a crowded place on campus, and he came to my dorm room once to chat and bring me takeout. He was all nice and…slick. *Slick*," she repeated. "I can see that now. The slickness covering the slimy person beneath. What I don't understand though is what made him snap like that when I told him I didn't want to go out with him. I have no idea what made him turn complete asshole stalker and the vicious killer."

Nash had given that plenty of thought, and he thought he had a theory. "I think it has to do with my mother and Bodie's relationship with our father."

He paused. Had to. Because it wasn't easy recalling all this shit from his past.

"Bodie was very close to my dad," Nash went on a moment later, and he took a turn to his place. "Ironic, since he was a sick, abusive bastard who beat my mother. Jericho, Slade, and me always tried to protect her. Not Bodie. He was always goading Dad on into keeping her in line when she'd mouth off."

"Keeping her in line by assaulting her," Caroline spelled out.

"Exactly. There was a dangerous misogynistic edge to both Bodie and my father. No respect for women. All whores, they'd say. Only good for one thing."

Yeah, not easy to pick at this scab.

Even now, all these years later, he could hear Bodie and his father snarling out that to his mother and any other female who had the misfortune of crossing paths with them.

"My dad and mom were arguing, and he pushed her into the creek," Nash explained. "I didn't see it. Jericho did though. And he tried to have our dad arrested, but no one in the compound where we were raised believed him."

Caroline stayed quiet for several long moments. "So, your father got away with murder."

"He did," Nash verified. "And I think Bodie always figured he could get away with it, too."

She made a sound of agreement. "Is your dad still alive?"

"I don't know," he had to admit. Then, he had to admit something else. "I haven't looked for him. He left the compound and disappeared."

Many, many times Nash had considered tracking him down and making him pay for what he'd done. But the truth was Nash wasn't certain he could confront the asshole without outright killing him. While the SOB deserved to die, Nash wasn't a murderer. He wasn't like the bastard. So, it was best to let sleeping dogs lie, at least until Nash was certain a visit like that wouldn't land him in jail.

"I'm sorry," Caroline said. "I guess we've both had our own life shitstorms."

They had indeed. And it was impossible for him to shove aside that shitstorm now that he'd brought it back to the surface. That was the problem with shitstorms. They kept coming at you. Worse, by having this conversation with

Caroline, her nightmarish memories were at the surface, too.

Or so he thought.

"Why didn't you come back and see me after we danced and hung out at that party?" she asked.

Nash definitely hadn't been expecting that turn in the conversation, and all he managed was a goofy-sounding "Uh."

"We had a connection," Caroline went on. "And don't say we didn't."

No way could he say that. The connection had indeed been there, along with a boatload of lust.

Both were still lingering around, too.

Since Nash didn't want to confirm that, he went with the obvious reason he hadn't contacted her. "I stayed away because my brother nearly killed you."

Caroline huffed. "It was my mother, wasn't it? That was the real reason." She stopped, muttered something under her breath that he didn't catch before she added, "My mother was the reason I didn't contact you," she admitted.

Nash shot her a quick glance but didn't question her on that. He just waited for her to continue. She did after she huffed.

"I didn't want to cause a rift between you and your boss. Something that I'm doing now," Caroline tacked onto that. "And I'm sorry. Probably not sorry enough though to put a stop to it."

Thankfully, Nash didn't have to respond to that since he took the final turn to his house, and they approached the security gate. He figured though that this conversation wasn't over. Nope. Caroline apparently wasn't going to hold back any of her feelings.

For now, anyway.

She might rethink those free flowing confessions once she was inside his place and had had some downtime to process everything that'd just happened. It had been an eventful hour and a half, that was for sure, and maybe it'd be the last of the eventfulness if Slade and the cops managed to catch Bodie.

Nash stopped at the gate and glanced around. Again, nothing seemed out of the ordinary. Like Caroline's, his place was off the beaten path as well and had once been a large horse ranch. Nash did keep a few horses, but it hadn't been the main reason he'd bought it. A much bigger buying point for him had been the potential to keep it secure. In his line of work, that was a necessity since he'd helped to put plenty of people behind bars. Sometimes, those asshole bad people got out and came looking for him.

Asshole bad guys like Bodie.

Except Bodie wasn't after him but rather Caroline.

That was a reminder that robbed Nash of any potential piece of mind.

"Oz, open the gate," he instructed, and the metal gates slid open. "There are motion sensors all over the property," he told her. "And the house itself has sensors on every window and door."

He hoped that would make her feel safe. Then again, feeling safe might not be possible for her, what with Bodie out there somewhere.

Nash drove toward the one-story stone and wood house and had Oz open the garage doors. Once he had the SUV inside, he gave Slade a wave, and his brother made an immediate turnaround. Heading back to join the hunt for Bodie.

"Wait until the garage door closes before you get out of the SUV," Nash instructed.

Caroline flinched a little. "Because Bodie could be nearby and watching the place."

That was always possible, but if so, he'd have to do it with long-range equipment since coming near the house would set off the sensors. Still, it was possible. And Nash thought of those photos of Caroline. The ones that'd been left in the bloodbath scene. Those had been taken long range so it was a skillset that either Bodie or someone he knew had.

"It's just a precaution to stay out of the line of sight of, well, someone who shouldn't have eyes on us," Nash settled for saying. Of course, they'd be taking many more precautions until this ordeal was over.

The moment the garage door touched down, he got out, leading her into the house. It wasn't a fancy place. Not his style. But he hadn't gone the bachelor pad mode either. His living room furniture was shades of blue and gray that coordinated with the kitchen colors in the open floorplan.

Emphasis on *open*.

The living, dining, kitchen, and his office area were all one big space. A well-lit one thanks to the skylights and the floor-to-ceiling windows in the kitchen and the east side of the living room. Those windows gave him amazing views of the pastures. Even now, he could see one of his Palominos grazing near the barn.

The bedrooms were all on the west side of the house. Three of them, each with its own amazing views.

"The windows and the skylights are bullet resistant," he explained. "And no one can see in."

Caroline went to the living room window to look out. "I see you like your privacy as much as I do," she muttered. "No neighbors. Lots of space."

"It's quiet," Nash agreed. "Comes in handy when I need to crash after a tough op."

"An op like this one," she said, looking at him from over her shoulder. "I'm the op this time."

He sighed, went to her. "Caroline, you're not an op for me."

She turned, studying his face, and then surprised him by smiling. "I think that's the most romantic thing you've ever said to me."

The comment seemed to make him stupid because he smiled, too. And added, "Then, obviously I haven't said enough romantic things."

Yeah, stupid all right.

But it'd felt so good to see her smile. What

didn't feel good was that look of fear still shimmering in her eyes. That look squeezed his gut into a tight ball. And it was that look and not his recent bout of stupid that caused him to pull Caroline into his arms.

Nash didn't intend to kiss her. Nope. No way. Because it was a line that he shouldn't cross. He crossed it anyway, though when she lifted her head, locking her gaze with his. That caused the heat to start firing on all cylinders, and despite that mental lecture he'd just given himself, he touched his mouth to hers.

Oh, man.

He was toast.

Burnt to a crisp toast.

Just that mere brush of his mouth over hers sent off alarm bells in his head. Bad alarms. Ones warning him to put his libido in check and move away from her.

That didn't happen though.

Just the opposite did.

He pressed harder with his mouth, and she made a sound of pleasure that robbed him of any willpower. Robbed him, too, of the last of his logical thoughts. Nash reacted all right. He reacted by sliding his tongue over her bottom lip. Tasting her. Letting that taste do the job it was obviously intended to do.

Make him forget all possible consequences.

Making him forget how to breathe.

Thankfully though, he didn't need actual

breath to go in for more. He pressed his mouth harder against hers, easing his tongue past her lips for a long, deep, slow kiss that fired through him.

His body seemed to think this was a prelude to sex. And that the sex should happen soon.

Thankfully, he was saved by the bell.

Or rather by his phone ringing.

That snapped back some of his control since it was a reminder that a lot of things were going on right now. Things that didn't involve kissing Caroline or his dick.

He moved away from her, taking out his phone in the same motion, and Nash frowned when he saw Unknown Caller on the screen. It could be spam.

But it could also be Bodie.

And that's why he answered it.

"McKenna," the caller snarled.

Not Bodie, but it was a voice he recognized. Leland Harris.

"Mr. Harris," Nash *greeted*. "What do you want?" He didn't use his polite voice either.

"I want my daughter, that's what," Leland was quick to growl out. "Where the hell is Jordana?"

Nash sighed. "I have no idea. The last time I saw her, she was with you. Why would you think I'd know where she is?"

"Because she left. She got in her car and just sped away when the cops were talking to me."

Hell.

Nash figured he'd be getting a call or text

about that soon, and sure enough, a message came in from Ruby to let him know that Jordana was missing. Ruby didn't think the woman could have gotten far, but the county deputy was issuing an APB for her.

"You think Jordana left to meet Bodie?" Nash came out and asked the man.

"No." He stopped, cursed. "But I guess that's her plan in a roundabout way." Leland spewed out even more profanity. "According to the note she left me, Jordana said she was going after Caroline."

CHAPTER EIGHT

———— ☆ ————

Caroline stepped from the shower and immediately looked out the window of the guest suite bathroom.

In the past sixteen or so hours since she'd arrived at Nash's, she'd been doing a lot of checking out the windows. A lot of listening, too, for any sounds of someone breaching Nash's elaborate security system.

But nothing so far.

It'd been a quiet night after what had been the day from hell. At the moment, it was a quiet morning, too, since there were no signs of Bodie or Jordana. Then again, Nash had assured her that they wouldn't be able to get close to the house without Oz letting him know.

Since no alarms had gone off during the night, Caroline hoped that meant Nash had gotten some sleep in his room across from hers. If he had, then that made one of them at least who'd managed to sleep. She certainly hadn't, but again, she hadn't expected it.

Because that long day from hell had stayed

with her.

Throughout the night, all those images and sounds had come rushing at her. Images of her bloody bedroom and those pictures. The stench and heat of the fire. The blasts from the bullets. All attempts to either rattle or kill her. And the incendiary device used to ignite the fire had come close to doing that since only minutes earlier, Nash, Ruby, and she had been in the house.

Caroline pushed that thought aside, something she'd been doing all night, but, of course, the reminder of that would return. It didn't stand a chance of starting to fade until Bodie was caught.

Which might happen today.

She had to cling to that hope. Cling hard. Had to also put her faith in her mother's team of operatives and the cops. They would find Bodie and Jordana, and the threat would end.

Bolstered a little by that hope, temporarily anyway, Caroline dressed in the clothes that Nash had arranged to be delivered by one of his co-workers. It wasn't a surprise that the underwear, jeans, and top fit her as if they were her own.

Probably thanks to Ruby's input.

Caroline would need to thank her mother for that later. Thank Ruby, too, for not putting up a fuss about her staying with Nash. Her mom probably thought seeing Nash would be like adding salt to a wound. It wasn't. More like balm to that particular wound.

Soothing, warm balm.

Along with an amazing kisser.

She doubted though that Nash would consider that kiss as a form of comfort. Or a wise move. And he'd be right about that last part.

The kiss hadn't been a particularly smart move since it was a distraction they didn't need. However, Nash and she seemed to be on a sexual collision course, fueled by an attraction that'd been there since she'd first laid eyes on him. It hadn't been love at first sight, but it had certainly been a powerful lust that didn't seem to want to be denied.

She made her way down the hall and found Nash exactly where she'd expected him to be. In his work area. Even though it was just past seven, he'd likely been at it for hours. Maybe even all night.

"There's coffee," Nash said, motioning toward the kitchen counter. He was reading something on his screen, obviously something that had snared his attention since he only glanced at her. "And I made some eggs and bacon. The plate's in the microwave."

"Thanks." No way could she eat, not with her stomach so unsettled, but she needed the caffeine to ease her throbbing headache.

"I didn't see Jordana or Bodie when I looked at the window," she remarked as she poured herself some coffee.

"No," he agreed. "No one's seen either of them." Now, he swiveled his chair around to face her.

And they both muttered some profanity.

"You didn't sleep," he said, just as she said, "Seriously? How the heck can you look this good with little to no sleep?"

The silence came, settling around them, and the corner of Nash's mouth lifted into a smile. "Your, uh, observation was more flattering than mine."

"You mean because your observation alluded to the fact that my eyes are bloodshot and I look like hell?"

"You could never look like hell," he countered.

Ah, the right thing to say. It made her want to kiss him. Then again, many things made her want to do that. But she saw something that stopped her.

A report on Jordana.

It was the one that Nash had no doubt been reading when she walked in, and she could immediately see why he'd been so engrossed with it.

"Jordana withdrew nearly a quarter of a million from her trust fund yesterday," Caroline read aloud. "And she owns two guns."

Nash made a sound of agreement and shifted back to the screen. "Guns she knows how to use. She's taken extensive firearms training."

"Not exactly the norm for someone in her social circle," Caroline muttered. "Then again, neither is marrying a convicted felon."

"No," he agreed. "And Bodie isn't Jordana's only

venture into the criminal world. She calls herself an investigative journalist, a crusader who fights injustice of those wrongfully convicted."

Caroline sighed, and without thinking—*definitely without thinking*—she lifted her top to show the scars on her stomach and chest. All eight of them were well healed now but still clearly visible as were the other three scars on her thighs.

Nash swallowed hard, and that's when the regret kicked in for her. She yanked the top back down.

"Sorry," she muttered just as he muttered, "I'm sorry."

So, once again, they were on the same wavelength. But this time, there was no smile. No heat in his eyes. Heat that she'd seen just for her. Now, there was bone-deep sympathy. The grief of what'd happened to her and what she'd lost of herself in the attack.

"No need for you to apologize," she managed. "Before yesterday, the scars weren't my number one thought."

Caroline paused and shifted the conversation to a better direction. "And the scars still aren't. No way for me to develop selective amnesia about Bodie's escape, but you're sort of sharing top billing in my head right now. FYI, your part of the top billing is good. I'm just glad you didn't apologize for that kiss," she spelled out to him.

"I was going to," he admitted. Now, he smiled just a little. "For what it's worth. You share top billing in my head, too."

He stood, went to her and eased her into his arms. Heck, this wasn't a got-to-have-you-now kind of embrace. It was because of those scars. Because it'd brought up the past for him, too. She had to remember that she wasn't the only one who'd been cut during the attack. She'd taken the physical brunt of it, yes, but they'd both been dealt a whopping mental blow.

She eased back a little to assure him of...well, anything that needed assurance, but their gazes locked. Just locked. And they stood there staring at each other.

Caroline drew in her breath, taking in his breath, too, since they were so close. So close that she caught his scent, too. It wasn't a scent found in a soap or a bottle. It was unique to Nash, and it stirred her.

Mercy, it did.

She moved toward him just as he moved toward her, and their mouths met, not for a comfort kiss. Nope. This was one of those got-to-have-you-now deals.

And the taste, the heat, the intensity roared through her.

He moved his mouth over hers as if he'd had tons of practice doing just this with her, and when he made the kiss French, this kicked up the urgency. Kicked up that aching need that was already spreading from her mouth to her center.

She'd never considered a single kiss to be

scalding hot foreplay, but this one was exactly that. A prelude that her body insisted could lead to even more scalding, hotter sex.

It didn't though.

Nash stepped back, and with his breath gusting, their gazes connected again. Her breathing wasn't so steady either, and certain parts of her were already whining about the kiss not continuing.

"Uh," she managed but had no idea how to finish that.

"Uh," he repeated, and he somehow worked up a smile even though she was pretty sure his body was burning as much as hers. "I think that proves just how much you're in my head, and I wish I could do something about that. More kissing, some touching," he added, surprising her with the admission. "I'd like to do both things with you. But there's this investigation, this hunt for Bodie. And I need to keep you safe. That has to take priority over kissing you."

"Are you sure about that?" she joked.

He smiled. Then, he sighed. "I'm sure." And Nash repeated it as if to convince himself before motioning to the report on the screen. "I'll read this and do my best to keep my hands off you."

So, he'd sneaked in an apology of sorts after all.

She added her own pseudo-apology by helping him get back that focus with a work-related question. "Anything else in that report I should know?" she asked. And this time, no matter what he said, she wouldn't be hiking up her top to show him those scars.

"Jordana has a history of helping felons," Nash explained, putting air quotes around helping. "So, Bodie wasn't her only venture into the criminal world. Sometimes, she pays legal fees for an inmate or uses her father's name to pressure prison officials into giving inmates certain privileges, like conjugal visits."

"Conjugal," she repeated, though it came out more like a hoarse whisper. "She had sex with Bodie?"

He nodded, and judging from the sudden tight set of his mouth, he was just as disgusted with that as she was. Caroline hadn't known that Bodie was a monster when she'd invited him into her life, but Jordana did. Of course, the woman thought he was innocent.

"So, how does Jordana's father feel about…all of this?" Caroline settled for saying.

"Serious disapproval. Serious," he emphasized. "Right before Bodie and she said I do, he tried to have her committed to a psychiatric hospital and declared mentally incompetent. Jordana fought it. Won. And then she seemed to have mended fences with her father for the whole ordeal. I think what really happened was that Leland decided to back off and keep his hatred of Bodie under wraps so he could work behind the scenes and put an end to the marriage."

Caroline gave that some thought. "Do you

think Leland actually set up Bodie's escape?"

"It's possible," Nash was quick to admit. "Leland has the means and motive, and he could have hired someone on the inside to set it up. Maybe he hoped Bodie would be gunned down at the prison or shortly thereafter." He paused a moment. "I seriously doubt he wanted Bodie to hook up with his daughter."

"No," she muttered, and Caroline had to shove aside something that flashed through her mind. That Bodie and Jordana had already hooked up.

And that Bodie had murdered her.

Caroline cleared her throat and had a huge gulp of coffee. "Where's Eddie?" she asked since she figured Nash had gotten an update on the man as well. Plus, this would get them off the topic of Jordana for a while.

Nash blew out a long, frustrated breath. "Not in jail where he belongs. His lawyer was able to convince the cops that he wasn't aiding and abetting Bodie, that he was merely trying to find him so he could talk him into surrendering. However, both Eddie and Leland will be interviewed by Detective Malley within the hour, and Malley's offered to let us watch the feed live."

"Oh, I want to watch," Caroline said. "I'm guessing Eddie has the money for a good lawyer?"

"Not at all. He's flat broke because his rich parents disowned him years ago, but someone paid top dollar for his lawyer. Ruby's looking into who did that."

Info like that might come in handy if it turned out Eddie was indeed helping Bodie.

"There was an update on the incendiary devices used on your house," Nash went on a moment later. "The bomb squad thinks accelerant pods were set around the perimeter of the back of your house. They were on timers. And there was a second one outside your workshop."

Well, damn it. That caused her heart to jump to her throat. "Did my workshop catch on fire?"

He shook his head. "The fire department disabled it."

That was something at least. All her work and equipment hadn't been destroyed like her house.

"The CSIs, who all survived the fire by the way, have also managed to find bits and pieces of what was left in your bedroom," he continued a moment later. "Everything will be examined."

His phone rang, cutting off whatever else he'd been about to say.

"Nash," Oz's voice said, pouring through the speaker on his computer. "Video call from Ruby. Should I put it through?"

"Absolutely." And Nash sat up straighter in his chair as her mother appeared on the large screen mounted on the wall.

"Nash," Ruby greeted. "Caroline. Any trouble there?"

"No," they said in unison.

"Good." She paused, looking at Caroline as if she had something else to say, but then she shifted her attention to her own laptop screen. "I just got some updates that I wanted to let you know about. As expected, Leland is pulling out all the stops to find Jordana, but so far, his team of PIs has come up with nothing. However, he told the cops that Bodie might kill Jordana so he can inherit her estate."

Nash cursed. "She didn't do a prenup?"

"Nope. And she's worth millions. Millions minus the two hundred thousand she withdrew yesterday," her mother tacked onto that. "If Jordana dies and if Bodie isn't convicted of her murder, then he'll become a very rich man."

"So, that might be the reason Bodie escaped," Nash muttered.

"Yes, and all the stuff that went on at Caroline's could have been a ruse. Something to cover up his real intentions of offing his wife and inheriting her estate." Ruby paused. "Though that would still leave Bodie with a big problem of having to go back to jail. Even if he wasn't convicted of Jordana's murder, he'd still have to face charges of escape and assaulting the nurse."

"Maybe he's planning on getting out of the country," Caroline suggested. "He could do that with the money Jordana's already withdrawn, and then he could try to tap into the rest later on."

Ruby made a sound of agreement and brought up something else on her laptop screen. A picture. But the angle was wrong for Caroline to make out who was in it. She hoped it wasn't another photo like those left in her bedroom.

"Another update," her mother said. "I've had some people scouring social media, traffic cams, and such for anything related to the investigation, and this popped up. It was taken at a party about six months ago and posted on social media. It's grainy because the photo wasn't focused on the couple but some other people. Still, facial recognition was able to pick it up, so I'm sending it to your screen now."

Seconds later, the image appeared, and, yes, it was indeed grainy. But Caroline had no trouble figuring out who the man and woman were.

"Crap," she spat.

"That was my reaction, too," her mother said. "And now, the question is, why was Jordana kissing Eddie Mulcrone less than a month before she married Bodie?"

CHAPTER NINE

———————— ☆ ————————

"Jordana and Eddie," Nash muttered, trying to wrap his head around that.

When Ruby, Caroline, and he were in the woods with Eddie, the man hadn't had favorable things to say about Jordana. Then again, Eddie had also claimed he'd been there to talk Bodie into turning himself in.

So, Eddie was a liar.

And apparently not very loyal to Bodie, someone he thought of as a brother, since the photo showed Eddie kissing a woman who would have been Bodie's fiancée at the time.

"Maybe Jordana is using Eddie," Caroline speculated. "Maybe she used sex to convince him to help her set up Bodie's escape."

Nash took a moment to process that and nodded. "That's a good angle." And it seemed more plausible than Jordana having the hots for Eddie.

But why would Eddie have gone along with it?

Would sex with his best friend's fiancée have been enough to convince him?

Nash immediately thought of kissing Caroline.

The heat and pleasure hadn't made him a complete idiot, but it had certainly clouded his head and made him burn for her even more. Maybe it was that way for Eddie.

"I've already sent a copy of this photo to Detective Malley, and I'll let you know when Eddie's and Leland's interviews start at SAPD headquarters," Ruby went on. "FYI, Slade should be there at your place any minute now. And full disclosure, I temporarily pulled him off the search for Bodie in the hopes that Bodie would follow him and that Slade would be able to intercept him along the route. Yes, it was a risk—"

"A good one," Nash interrupted. "Because if Bodie comes here, Slade and I can catch him."

Ruby seemed to breathe a whole lot easier. "I figure Bodie knows where you live, but he could see Slade as his ticket to getting inside your place. He's not. Slade thoroughly checked his van to make sure Bodie hadn't stashed himself inside it. But it's still possible that Bodie has managed to track where Slade is going and is keeping him under surveillance."

It was especially doable if Jordana had shelled out some of her money for equipment to allow Bodie to do that. And at this point, they had to assume there was a good chance that Jordana and Bodie had hooked up and she had given him whatever he needed. Also, if Jordana had indeed helped him with his escape, then she likely would have set up a safe, off the grid place for them to go to minimize the chance of Bodie being recaptured.

"Anyway, Slade will be there soon to drop off some more items, including Caroline's meds and some groceries. I figured you hadn't had a chance to shop in between your last mission and getting to Caroline's."

"I hadn't," Nash said. Then, he stopped and added. "Caroline's meds?" He looked at her for an explanation.

"Low-dose antibiotics," Caroline told him. "I've been on them since, well, since the attack. My spleen had to be removed, and that means I'm more suspectable to catching stuff and getting an infection."

Hell. He hadn't known that, and Nash immediately glanced at the small nicks and burns she'd gotten from the explosion.

"I'm fine," Caroline insisted, obviously noticing that he was giving her the once-over.

Clearly, she wasn't fine if she had needed meds for all this time, but Nash didn't press as to why she hadn't told him about this earlier, especially since the pressing wouldn't accomplish squat. Instead, he turned back to Ruby, thanked her for the updates, and ended the call just as he heard a series of beeps.

"Oz, security monitor on," Nash instructed.

Within a blink, the feed from multiple security cameras popped up on the blank screen where Ruby's image had just been. And he saw Slade's van at the security gate. Since his brother already had the code, the gate opened and Slade drove in.

"He'll be pissed that he hasn't found Bodie," Nash let Caroline know.

One look at Slade's face and Nash had confirmation of what he'd just said. He could see Slade scowling. The scowl didn't let up either as he used the code to open the garage and park his van inside.

Several moments later, Slade came in through the mudroom, and he was carrying several large plastic bags.

"Oz, reset all security," Nash instructed, nodding a greeting to his brother.

Slade's scowled managed to get even worse. "Oz? What happened to Caroline?"

Nash groaned just as Caroline gave Slade a wide-eyed stare. "Nothing else happened to me. Why?"

"No, not you..." Slade's words trailed off when he noticed the look on Nash's face. A look that obviously conveyed that he wished Slade hadn't said anything about this.

"My AI app," Nash clarified because he had to say something. "I used to call it Caroline."

She smiled, which was a far better reaction than Nash had considered she might have. "Did it have my voice?" she asked.

Nash nodded, cursed under his breath. "I know that must sound creepy."

Still smiling, Caroline lowered her head and shook it. "No, it sounds...promising. Like maybe you didn't forget about me after that party."

"I'd never forget about you," Nash muttered before thinking that through.

He should have thought it through.

This time, it was Slade who groaned. "Okay, I don't see any pitfalls with what's going on here." There was so much sarcasm in his voice. "No possible lack of objectivity. No potential to piss off the boss. No—"

"I know," Nash interrupted, and then he did a quick change of subject. "You brought Caroline her meds?"

That caused Slade's scowl to return, and he set all but one of the bags on the kitchen counter. He handed the last one to Caroline. "Meds and some extra toiletry items that Ruby recommended."

Caroline looked inside the bag and sighed. "It's hard to stay completely furious with her when she does thoughtful things like this," she muttered under her breath. Then, she winced as if she'd said too much.

Nash was right there with her. He'd taken the *too much said* dive as well. So had Slade by bringing up the AI app formerly known as Caroline.

Slade checked the feed from the security cameras that was still on the monitor, and he cursed. "The sonofabitch didn't follow me. And I gave him ample opportunity for it. I mean, if he was watching me at the grocery store, he'd likely know I wasn't buying lavender shampoo for me. Added to that, the antibiotics script is in Caroline's name."

Yeah, that would have given Bodie or Jordana some clues as to where Slade would be heading with those items.

"You didn't get a sense of anyone following you?" Caroline asked.

Slade didn't do what Nash thought he might—grumble at her for something Slade would take as an insult. Because Slade wouldn't have had to rely on "a sense" for that sort of thing. He would have spotted anyone tailing him.

"No one followed me," Slade assured her. "No one put a tracker on my van. And no one got in my field of vision to alert me that I was being watched."

"Maybe because Bodie didn't need to watch or follow you," Nash pointed out. "Any one at Caroline's yesterday could likely figure out I brought her here with me. Anyone, including Jordana."

"Yeah," Slade agreed. "So, what the hell is the fucker waiting on? Unless his IQ has dropped to subpar level while he's been in jail, he has to know Caroline's not just going to serve herself up to him on a silver platter." He shifted toward Caroline. "You're not going to do that, right?"

"I'm not," she confirmed and then paused. "But like you, I want him caught. If Bodie won't come here because of the tight security, then maybe I go someplace where he thinks he can come at me. Sort of like your trip to the grocery store to buy lavender shampoo."

Nash did some cursing. Slade, however, nodded in approval. At first anyway. He quit the nodding when he saw Nash's reaction.

"A silver platter with a crapload of protection," Slade spelled out. "That could work, but I'm guessing neither Nash nor Ruby will go for that."

"I won't," Nash was quick to say. "I think it's best if we stick to the plan and keep looking for Jordana and Bodie."

Slade shrugged again, just as his phone dinged with a text. So did Nash's.

"It's from Ruby," Nash relayed to Caroline. "The interview with Eddie is starting."

He sent a reply to thank Ruby. Then, he instructed Oz to tap into the feed link that Ruby had sent him. It took only a couple of seconds for the link to load, and the feed came on the screen.

Detective Malley and another cop were on one side of the interview table, and Eddie and a guy in a suit were across from him. Eddie's lawyer, no doubt. As standard procedure, Malley read in the date, time, case number, and the names of all of those present.

"Ruby's already doing a run on the lawyer," Slade let them know, though he added the name to a memo on his phone. Gary Sullivan.

Nash made note of it, too, since he wanted to do his own deep dive on the lawyer and find out who was footing the bill. And why.

"Mr. Mulcrone, I need to inform you that this

interview is being recorded. And as I explained to you earlier, several people are watching, including my lieutenant." Malley pointed to the camera on the wall. "Do you wish to know the names of those observers, and do you need me to reread your rights to you?"

"My client understands his rights," Sullivan interjected. "And even though I would prefer to have no one listening in, my client has instructed me that he doesn't wish to object to that matter. Therefore, he doesn't need the names of those observers. Also, my client wishes to make a statement at this time."

Malley kept a blank face while he nodded, and Eddie picked up a piece of paper. A statement the lawyer had likely had a big hand in creating.

"I, Eddie Mulcrone, did not assist Bodie McKenna in any way in his escape. I have no idea where he is, and if he contacts me, I fully intend to try to convince him to turn himself in."

"Uh huh," Malley said, not sounding the least bit convinced. "And did you try to convince Bodie when he called you and asked you to meet him in the woods near Miss Maverick's residence?"

"He didn't give me the chance," Eddie readily answered. "He just asked me to meet him there."

"And he did that so you could take him money, a phone, and a knife that you had with you," Malley countered.

Eddie wasn't so quick to answer this time. He looked at his lawyer, who answered for him.

"Those were all my client's personal items. He had no intentions of giving them to the escapee."

"Uh huh," Malley repeated. "That isn't what your client told Ruby Maverick, Caroline Maverick, and Nash McKenna when the three of them found him in the woods."

"My client was rattled," the lawyer insisted, not missing a beat. "Terrified actually since those three were heavily armed and had a menacing presence. My client misspoke, but he never intended to help the escapee. That would be against the law," he tacked onto that.

"Yeah, it would," Malley muttered and leaned back in his chair. "So, help me with some insight here about Bodie, since you consider him like a brother and all. Is Bodie the jealous sort?"

Ah, Nash knew where this was going, but Eddie and the lawyer just looked confused by the question.

"I mean, is Bodie jealous of Jordana?" Malley spelled out when neither Eddie nor the lawyer responded.

The confusion left Eddie's face. "No." He sighed and leaned forward as if telling a secret. "Look, Bodie married Jordana for her money. And the sex. That's it. But he doesn't love her. He still has a thing for Caroline."

From the corner of his eye, Nash saw Caroline flinch, and he automatically moved closer to her. Hell. That was not something Nash had wanted to hear.

"Caroline, the woman Bodie tried to murder?" Malley commented.

"Yeah, her." Eddie shrugged. "I don't get it. I mean, she's a looker all right, but it's like Bodie's obsessed with her. She's the one who rejected him and all. The one he loved, and she threw that love back in his face."

Caroline didn't step away from Nash. Didn't take her attention off the screen. But this had to feel like multiple hard blows.

"So, Bodie would be jealous of Caroline but not his wife?" Malley asked.

"Absolutely," Eddie declared with total conviction.

Malley opened a folder and took out the picture. "Then Bodie wouldn't care about you kissing his wife." He slid the photo toward the two men.

Every drop of color vanished from Eddie's face. "Fuck," he muttered.

His lawyer immediately clamped onto his arm. "Don't say another word," he warned Eddie.

"I like that old saying," Detective Malley threw out there. "You know, the one about a picture being worth a thousand words. And what a picture this is. If you look real close, you can see that Jordana is wearing the engagement ring she bought for Bodie to give her."

"It was a mistake," Eddie blurted, and he shook off the lawyer's grip. "A mistake," he added. "Jordana came onto me, and I gave in. It was stupid, yes, and I instantly regretted it."

"Jordana came onto you," Malley remarked, again with loads of skepticism. "Why would she do that when she was engaged?"

Eddie seemed to wither some under Malley's suddenly intense stare. "I don't know. You'd have to ask her. Personally, I think she did it because she was jealous of Bodie and me. Because Bodie and I were so close, and I think she wanted to put a wedge between us."

"Uh huh," Malley reacted. "And did she tell Bodie about this, uh, one off or whatever the heck it was?"

"No," Eddie snapped, and a few seconds later, he repeated it in a mutter. "I don't want Bodie to know either. There's no reason for it."

"My client and I need a moment," the lawyer interrupted. "Cut the camera," he said, looking up at it. "I don't want you or your audience listening in on this."

Malley nodded, stood and pressed something in the keypad next to the door. The screen immediately went blank.

Nash was thankful for the reprieve since he wanted to check on Caroline. That didn't happen though. He'd barely made it a step toward her when his phone dinged with another text. Probably Ruby, wanting to see how Caroline was doing as well.

But it wasn't.

Unknown Caller was on the screen.

"Maybe Leland again," he muttered, and he opened the text.

And he cursed.

"What's wrong?" Caroline and Slade asked in unison.

Nash's gaze froze on the words, and he wished he didn't have to tell her. But he couldn't keep this from her. Even if seeing it was going to cut Caroline to the bone.

He held up his phone so she could read what was written there.

"Hello, darlin'," she read aloud, her voice barely a whisper. "Watch the attached video for an important message."

"I can have the video screened," Nash was quick to say. "To check it for a virus." Though he figured Bodie wouldn't do that since he'd want Caroline to see it.

So he could taunt her.

And terrorize her.

"Play the video," she insisted.

Nash debated it, and hoping it wasn't a mistake, he loaded it onto the monitor so they could all watch.

Bodie instantly appeared on the screen, and Nash tried not to react to the gut punch of hatred that he had for this bastard. Impossible not to react though since Bodie was sporting that same grin as he had in the photo that'd been left in Caroline's bedroom.

His brother's black hair fell nearly to his

shoulders, and his easy, careless expression made him look like some kind of seasoned rock star. He still had his looks, looks that he'd obviously used to convince Jordana to marry him.

Nash paused the frame so he could study Bodie's surroundings to try to figure out where he'd been when this was recorded. But there was nothing to study. Bodie was sitting in front of what appeared to be a white bed sheet that had been nailed to a wall.

"Caroline," Bodie purred when the video started up again. "I have so much to say to you. I really hope you're having a miserable time right now, what with looking over your shoulder for me."

"You sick sonofabitch," she muttered.

Bodie laughed, maybe anticipating a more terrified reaction from her. "Now that I'm a free man, we'll be connecting really soon." He held up something.

A skinning knife.

"The cops took my other one," Bodie went on. "But as you can see, I have a new one."

Bodie ran the blade over his tongue and then turned back to the camera. Now, he was sporting a stone-cold glare. "Can't wait to slice this right into you," he growled. "This time, bitch, you'll die."

CHAPTER TEN

———— ☆ ————

Caroline watched as the video ended, and she welcomed the emotions that rolled through her. Not fear. Definitely not that. What she felt was an intense, raw anger that shot through every part of her.

She darn sure wouldn't be crying this time. Wouldn't be going through that sickening dread as she'd done when she had learned that Bodie had escaped and was coming after her. Feeling that was over and done.

And now she was ready to fight.

"Text that sick SOB back and tell him to bring it on," she snarled.

Nash closed his eyes for a second, and while he didn't come out and sigh, that's what he looked as if he wanted to do. Sigh and figure out a way to convince her not to throw down this kind of gauntlet.

"Leland was right to try to use me to draw him out," she went on because clearly she had some convincing to do. "And what's not right is for Bodie to hide like the chickenshit coward that he is and taunt me like this."

"No, it's not right," Nash agreed. "But you have to see beyond what you want to do to this ass and try to think of why he would have done something like this."

The answer seemed obvious to her. "He did it because he's a sick bastard, and he wanted to terrorize me and send me into an emotional tailspin."

"Maybe that's what he had in mind," Nash conceded, "but it seems, well, unnecessary to taunt you. So, what could he gain from doing it?"

"Or what could *someone else* gain from it?" Slade put in. He paused, and when he had Caroline's attention, he continued. "It could be a distraction, plain and simple. We start chasing our tails, focusing on things like trying to triangulate the locations of the texter. But that will be a big-assed waste of time since it'll be a burner phone, and I'm betting the sender is no longer in that area. He hit send and then got the hell out of dodge."

Yes, that made sense. But Caroline wasn't going to rule out that Bodie had done all of this as a round of mental torture. Warped bastards liked to do warped things.

"I'll let Ruby know about the text and video," Slade commented, taking out his own phone and stepping to the side.

That would no doubt put her mother on even more alert. If that was possible. At the moment it felt as if there were no more precautions to take.

Nothing left but the waiting.

And at the end of that wait, Caroline figured all of this would snowball into a showdown. She was ready for it. Mentally and physically. But Nash and her mother wouldn't see it that way. Their goal was to keep her out of harm's way even when the harm's way felt inevitable.

While Slade fired off that text, she moved to the window to look out at that amazing view. To see if there was a killer lurking around. But she saw no one. Even the horses weren't out and about this morning.

"How far out are your sensors?" Caroline asked, glancing over her shoulder at Nash.

He was at the monitor, studying the feed from the various security cameras. "They cover the perimeter of all ten acres."

A lot of space. Maybe too much. Was that a weak spot that Bodie could capitalize on?

"Can they be tampered with?" she pressed.

"Anything can be tampered with," Nash admitted. "But it won't be easy."

Still, it was possible, and she tried to think like a killer with some resources. It was possible Jordana had bought Bodie whatever equipment he needed to bypass those sensors.

But why would Jordana do that?

Why would the woman make it easy for her man to come after his obsession? Especially when that obsession was another woman?

Maybe it was a simple case of Jordana being

willing to do anything for her *husband*. Including having a one off with his friend to elicit some kind of cooperation from Eddie. That made sense in a warped way, and if so, Jordana could have arranged for other help for Bodie, for other supplies.

Caroline was in such deep thought that she gasped when the sound shot through the room. But it was only another alert for a text message. For a couple of heart-racing moments, she thought it might be another taunt from Bodie. It wasn't.

"Ruby says the interview with Leland is about to start," Nash relayed. "Eddie is still consulting with his lawyer."

Oh, to be a fly on the wall for that consult. The lawyer was likely trying to figure out how to put the right spin on the BS his client had been spouting about his innocence.

She turned so she could continue to keep watch and see the screen where Detective Malley and Leland appeared. Leland had three lawyers with him, and she was guessing he wouldn't be doing any talking because he was sitting back from the table with his arms folded over his chest. He clearly wasn't happy to be there.

Malley was in the process of reading Leland the Miranda Warning when there were more sounds. Not the dinging from a text either. But a piercing set of beeps that seemed to have an urgency to them.

Both Nash's and Slade's heads whipped up.

Both drew their guns.

"Move away from the window," Nash told her.

The words had barely had time to leave his mouth when the bullet slammed into the glass.

Gasping and choking back a scream, Caroline staggered back, automatically steeling herself up to feel the pain from the shot. But it didn't come. Then, she remembered Nash saying the glass was bullet-resistant.

Resistant.

Not bulletproof.

Which meant shots could get through.

Nash hurried to her, pulling her even further away. "Slade, do you see the shooter?" he asked.

Slade's response was drowned out because another round slammed into the glass, rattling it and causing it to crack and spread out like a spider's web.

Oh, God.

The glass wasn't going to hold.

Her anger was still there. Mercy, was it. But she also didn't want Nash or Slade hurt because their idiot brother was trying to kill her.

"The gunman's in a tree at the back of your property, just inside the fence," Slade spelled out, and he motioned toward the spot on the monitor to show the position.

Caroline couldn't actually see anyone. Not at first anyway. Then the morning sun glinted off the barrel of a rifle.

A third shot came, slamming into the spot

where the first two had landed.

"He's using armor-piercing bullets," Nash said. He looked at her and added, "When the glass stops the outer shell, there's an internal projectile that continues into the target."

Slade took up the rest of the explanation. "Yeah, and my guess is when the gunman creates a hole, he's going to send something else through. Maybe tear gas. Maybe something more lethal."

That didn't help her galloping heartbeat or the tight pressure in her chest that was vising her lungs and making it hard to breathe. And it caused another wave of guilt to wash over her. Bodie could kill his brothers to get to her.

"Maybe it's time for me to be that bait," she suggested.

"No," Nash and Slade said in unison.

Nash spared her another glance, one that told her there was nothing she could say or do to convince him to save Slade and himself. The bullets didn't convince him either. Not the fourth one. Not the fifth either.

And the shots just kept on coming.

"Oz, alert Ruby and 911 of the attack. Continue to monitor the security feed and report any movement of the intruder to me," Nash instructed while he went into the mudroom and brought back Kevlar vests and some more guns. He tossed one of the vests to her. "I'll be monitoring the feed on my phone."

"From where?" she asked while she put on the

vest.

"In Slade's van," Nash provided, donning his own vest. "There's more room in it than my SUV, and you'll be flat down in the back while Slade drives us through the pasture toward this asshole."

Caroline was sure she blinked because she certainly hadn't expected him to say that. "We're going to the shooter?" she had to ask.

"We're going to the shooter," Nash confirmed. "I'm not leaving you here where he could send some dangerous shit through that window. Let's move."

They did. Just as another shot tore through the glass, leaving a jagged plate-sized hole. Nash didn't wait around to see what the shooter would be sending through it. They just hurried into the garage.

The moment they were all inside the van and she was on the floor in the back, Nash used a voice command to open the garage door and he took off, practically flying backwards as he reversed out.

There were no windows in the back of the van which meant Caroline couldn't see squat. She figured though that bullets would have a harder time getting through the metal sides than the glass. So, she was a lot more protected than Nash and Slade were since their only buffer was the windshield. It was probably bullet-resistant, but she'd just seen that wasn't a surefire way to keep from being shot.

Even though they were no longer in the garage,

she could still hear the sound of gunfire behind them, a barrage now that was no doubt tearing its way through the rest of the living room window.

"I'm going faster," Slade muttered. "Just in case the shooter's about to fire an explosive into the house."

Oh, God. She hadn't considered that. But she should have after what'd happened to her own place. Not an explosive there, of course, but she figured there was a possibly that whatever came flying through the window could do just as much damage.

"What happens when we get closer to the shooter?" Caroline had to ask.

"Slade stops. I get out and use the van door for cover, and I give this asshole a taste of his own medicine," Nash said.

Her head whipped up enough so she could see he had his attention pinned to his phone, where he was no doubt watching the security feed.

"The vest won't protect you from a headshot," she said, using what he'd told her when they'd been under attack back at her place.

Nash glanced back at her. "I'll take a calculated risk."

"We both will," Slade volunteered. "Because I'll be doing the same on the driver's side. I doubt the shooter will be firing much if he had two sets of ammo coming right at him."

Hopefully, that was true. But there was another factor that could play into this. They had no idea if

Bodie, or the shooter, was working alone.

Nash used a voice command to open the pasture gates, and she felt Slade slow the van before he sped up again. Obviously, there was no more driveway since they began to bobble around on the uneven ground.

She held her breath, waiting for the sound of an explosion. But it didn't come. However, more gunfire did. Not aimed at the house this time.

But rather at the van.

The bullets pinged off the metal, and she prayed they didn't ricochet and hurt one of Nash's horses. Or anyone else who happened to be in the area since they weren't that far from a road.

Slade slammed on the brakes just as the shots stopped, and both Nash and he cursed.

"What happened?" she asked.

But they didn't answer. They both just bolted from the van, and she braced herself for the sound of more gunfire. This time from Nash and Slade.

Everything went quiet though.

Too quiet.

"The sonofabitch is getting away," Slade spat out.

No, no, no. That was not what she wanted to hear. If he got away, there'd just be another attack. Another hellish wait to put an end to this.

"Stay here with Caroline," she heard Nash say. That caused her heart to drop. So did what Nash added next. "I'm going after him."

CHAPTER ELEVEN

———— ☆ ————

While silently cursing, Nash did a zigzag sprint toward the tree where he'd last seen the shooter. Cursing because he sure as hell wasn't seeing him now. And since the SOB wasn't firing any shots, that likely meant he was well on his way to being long gone.

Nash made it to the fence and scrambled over it, dropping down to the other side and immediately bringing up his gun.

Ready to fire.

But there was no blasted target.

He stopped, went still, and just listened. For a spring morning, it was plenty quiet. No birds. No rustle of wind. No running footsteps. Hell. Did that mean Bodie or whoever had fired those shots had dropped down and was lying in wait?

Maybe.

But Nash didn't get a sense of that. In fact, his instincts were telling him he was alone here. So, where the hell had he gone?

And was it even a *he*?

No way to know if it was Bodie. Or Eddie. But it could be Jordana, too, especially since she'd had all that firearms training. Shit, for that matter, it could be some minion they'd hired to do their bidding. Someone willing to put a bullet in Caroline.

Someone willing to kill her.

Nash got moving again, taking slow, cautious steps. Still listening. And still hearing nothing.

Not at first anyway.

But then he caught a sound and did more cursing. Because it was a motorcycle engine, and it was coming from a good thirty yards away.

Nash took off running, watching for any IEDs or traps that the shooter might have left behind. This wasn't his property, so there were no sensors or cameras to detect someone doing that sort of thing, and if the shooter knew that, he or she might have decided to capitalize on the security flaw.

He bolted through the woods, following the sound of the engine. But the motorcycle was moving, too, getting further and further away from him. Nash didn't catch sight of it until he made it all the way to the road. Even then, he got just a glimpse, a blur of motion, before the rider sped around a curve and out of sight.

"Oz, alert Ruby," he said, turning and running back toward the van. "The shooter escaped, heading east on Anderson Road on what I think is a black and silver Harley. Deploy a drone."

While Oz took care of that, Nash ran back to the van as fast as he could. Because it occurred to him that with the direction the shooter was heading, he or she would be going directly past the road to Nash's place. The SOB could take the turn and try to go after Caroline again. She was with Slade, who'd protect her, but Nash didn't want them to face this potential threat without the extra help he could give them.

"Since Oz is still connected to the dash monitor, I heard what you told the app," Slade said as Nash approached the van.

Obviously, Caroline had heard it, too, because she was sitting up enough for him to see her face. And for him to notice the fresh dread that was there. Nash wanted to make the shooter pay for that look. For the fear she had to be feeling.

"I'm sorry," Nash told her when he got in the van.

She didn't have quite the reaction he'd expected. Caroline hooked her hand around the back of his neck and kissed him. Not a gentle one either. It was rather hard and filled with the emotions that he'd seen in her expression.

And more.

Apparently, it had some relief in the mix, too.

Relief and so much pleasure.

That kick of pleasure came, sliding through him as her tongue slid over his mouth. Her taste was an instant balm, soothing. Arousing.

Perfect.

But it didn't last. Nope. She stopped it as quickly as she'd started it and pulled back to face him.

"Don't do that again," Caroline snapped. "Don't go running off after a killer like that. We could have driven the van closer so you wouldn't have been out in the open for nearly as long as you were. I want to punch you on the arm right now," she tacked onto that.

Despite everything they'd just been through, he had to fight a smile. Yeah, she'd been given another mental blow, but she'd taken the punch and had seemingly rolled with it.

"Yeah, this lust thing between you two won't interfere with anything," Slade grumbled, throwing the van into gear and turning around to start back toward the house.

The house that might or might not be habitable. Somehow that thought made it through the haze that the kiss had created and into Nash's mind. So did what Slade had just said.

"This *lust thing* won't interfere with me making Caroline's safety my top priority," Nash assured him.

Slade made a sound that could have meant anything. Or nothing. "All right, that's my priority, too, which is why I'm going to insist the two of you stay in the van while I go inside the house and check it out."

"You could wait for the cops," Caroline said,

and then she looked at Nash. "We heard what you told Oz to do, and since that means Oz and my mother have already alerted the cops. A county deputy or two should be here soon."

"In theory," Slade agreed. "But a lot of the county LEOs are tied up with the search for Bodie, so it might take them a while. Especially now since they'll also be looking for that motorcycle."

Slade was right. And Nash preferred them out looking for Bodie. The sooner they found him, the sooner Caroline would be out of danger.

The moment that Slade made it back to the garage and opened it, he drove in and immediately shut the door behind them.

"Wait here," Slade muttered. "And maybe talk or something instead of... hell." He waved that off. "Go ahead and kiss. You're obviously both brainless when it comes to each other."

They were, but Nash knew he was going to do a better job of... He stopped, looked at her and brushed his mouth over hers.

"After this is over, I won't keep my distance from you," Nash assured her.

"Progress," she muttered with her mouth still against his. "And this isn't a comfort kiss, is it? I mean, this feels like more than that."

"It is more," he assured her. "A whole lot more."

The timing sucked to spell that out, and saying it certainly didn't solve any of their problems. Just the opposite. But he knew this particular kiss wasn't going to lead to a heavy make-out session.

Or even another kiss. Not when he had to keep an ear out for anything Slade had to report.

There was also that possibility of Bodie or the shooter doubling back.

All of his security measures were still in place, but the shooter had found a way around that. Well, sort of. He or she had triggered the sensors, which had done their job of alerting Nash, but by staying at the far back of the fence, the gunman had managed to stay out of immediate range while still being able to fire what could have been killing blows.

If he or she had gotten lucky, that is.

That first shot had come right at Caroline when she'd been standing by the window, and if the specialized bullet had hit at the wrong angle or on some flawed spot of the glass, she could have been killed. Had that been the shooter's intention? Or had this attack been all about terrorizing her?

He hoped the drone would spot the motorcycle so they could catch the bastard, and then Nash could maybe find out the answer to that question.

"Oz, put the feed for the security cameras on the van's dash monitor," Nash instructed.

It was overkill information since the motion detectors would alert him if anyone came onto the grounds, but it wouldn't hurt to have a backup to those sensors.

Within seconds, the feed popped onto the dash, and as expected, Nash didn't see anyone. The gates were still closed, just as they should be, and he wouldn't be opening them until the cops had arrived. Even then, he'd verify every single one of them before letting them in. Because he wouldn't put it past Bodie to try to sneak in with the first responders.

The mudroom door opened, and Nash's hand automatically tensed on his gun, but it was only Slade.

"No one's inside," Slade reported. He had the bags he'd brought over earlier and stashed them on the console.

"There's the stench of some tear gas still lingering around, but other than that and the obvious broken window, that's it," Slade went on. "No other damage. The tear gas canister didn't even hit or break anything when it landed. It's just lying on the floor, ready for the CSIs to examine it and hopefully get a print that the dickhead shooter might have missed when he loaded it into the launcher."

Yeah, that was the hope, all right.

"The drone has something to report," Oz informed them, and the security feed was replaced with some other images. Not footage but rather a series of still photos that the drone had obviously shot.

Like Caroline and Slade, Nash looked at the pictures, but it didn't take a long study for him to spot what the drone had picked up.

A motorcycle.

Not on the road but rather in the ditch, and

there was no rider on or near it.

"Oz, where were these images taken?" Nash asked.

"A quarter of a mile from here," Oz promptly replied. "The motorcycle is within twenty feet of an old ranch trail."

A trail where the shooter had no doubt left a vehicle for his or her quick getaway.

"Ruby and the police have been alerted about this new information," Oz went on.

Good, and that meant the CSIs would examine the motorcycle for any prints or trace evidence. Nash wasn't hopeful they'd find anything, but again, they could get lucky. The shooter might have carefully planned this, but that didn't mean he or she hadn't made a mistake.

There was a series of beeps, and without Nash even having to give the command, Oz replaced the drone pictures with the live feed from the security cameras. Nash expected to see cops, lots and lots of them.

But this was a single vehicle.

And it sure as heck wasn't a cop driving it.

Hell in a handbasket. What was *she* doing here?

CHAPTER TWELVE

———— ☆ ————

"Jordana," Caroline grumbled when she saw the woman approach the gate in her silver Mercedes.

And Caroline's mind began to whirl with one big question.

Had Jordana been the one to fire those shots?

She certainly had the training for it, and she was obviously close by. The woman could have shot at them, ran when she spotted the van coming at her, then ditched the motorcycle and driven here to the gate.

But for what?

To try to finish what she'd started by shooting at them. Maybe. Caroline wouldn't put it past her since Jordana had already spouted how much she loved her husband, and if the love was true blue, then Jordana might indeed be willing to carry out this attack for Bodie.

"Oz, put the camera feed from the gate on the dash and open audio," Nash instructed. "I won't be letting in our visitor, but I definitely want to hear what she has to say."

So did Caroline, though if Jordana had enough nerve to have orchestrated that attack, she probably wouldn't be blurting out anything that would incriminate her. Or Bodie. But maybe there was something else that could be used to prove she was guilty.

"Can her clothes be checked for gunshot residue?" Caroline asked as she watched Jordana inch her car closer and closer to the gate.

"She can be, but since the shots came from a rifle, there might not be any," Nash said. "The barrel of the rifle is far enough away from the hands to keep them clean from the GSR."

"And she would have likely worn gloves," Slade pointed out. "Along with changing her clothes."

Yes, she would, especially if she'd had her car stashed near where that motorcycle had been left. Jordana likely would have also discarded any clothes that could possibly incriminate her.

Jordana drove up level with the intercom box and lowered her window. "Nash, I need to talk to you," she insisted.

Her tone was more than a little frantic. Then again, that had been her default mode back at Caroline's house. That and some anger. Caroline wasn't seeing much anger now, but the woman looked...shaken.

From what though?

The shooting?

Or was this because the cops were after her?

Maybe there was nothing the cops could use to arrest her if there was no evidence to link her to Bodie's escape and the attacks. However, Jordana had left the scene shortly after the fire at Caroline's house, and the cops might be able to charge Jordana with something related to that.

But Caroline immediately rethought that.

Her daddy's lawyers would fight such a charge. She was positive about that. But walking away a free woman didn't mean she was innocent.

"Nash?" Jordana called out again and used the back of her hand to wipe away tears. Judging from the mascara streaks on her cheeks, these weren't the only recent tears the woman had shed. "Please answer. Please."

Nash did something to the settings on his phone. "She'll be able to hear us but not see us," he let Slade and her know, and he answered the woman's *please*. It probably wasn't the answer Jordana wanted to hear, though. "Did you just try to kill us?" he came out and asked.

"No," she was quick to answer, and she added a fair amount of shock to her expression. Fake shock perhaps. "No, of course not," Jordana insisted. "Did someone try to kill you?"

Nash huffed. "What do you want, Jordana? Why are you here?"

A sob tore from her throat. "I got a call from Bodie, and he said someone was trying to kill him. Oh, God." More sobbing. "He was so scared that someone might try to kill him. I can't let him die. I

123

have to try to save him."

Even though Jordana couldn't see him, Nash aimed an eyeroll at the monitor. "The cops are indeed after him," Nash verified. "Maybe your father, too. So, yeah, he has a right to be worried that someone might end up shooting him. He could always just turn himself in to prevent that from happening."

"That's what I'm going to try to talk him into doing," Jordana quickly agreed. "Giving himself up so he can live. That's why I need to find him. Has he been here? Has he contacted Caroline?"

Caroline saw the debate that Nash was having with himself as to what to say. He could withhold info about that text and video. Or he could lay it out there and see how Jordana reacted.

"Bodie texted Caroline," Nash finally said. "He called her darlin'."

Well, that got a reaction from the woman, all right. Jordana let out a loud shriek, and she bashed the palm of her hand against the steering wheel. "He promised me he was over her, that she meant nothing to him. It's not right. It's not fair. He's married to me. He's my husband." By the time she reached that last bit, she was screaming out the words.

"I'm surprised you're so jealous of him," Nash commented. "I mean, since you had an affair with your husband's best friend."

Jordana's head whipped sideways, and her stony gaze fired straight into the camera. "That sonofabitch Eddie. He told you we'd had an affair. We didn't," she spat out.

"I have a photo of the two of you kissing," Nash added. "The cops have a copy of it, too, and they've questioned Eddie about it."

She shrieked again and did more hand banging against the steering wheel. If she kept it up, she was going to risk breaking some bones.

"It's all falling apart," Jordana cried out. "It wasn't supposed to be like this. Bodie and I were supposed to be…somewhere else." Unlike before, her voice got softer as she continued to speak until she was trailing off into a barely audible whisper. "We were supposed to be living our lives together."

The crying picked up pace, and Jordana was now gulping in large, hiccupping breaths. But that stopped when there was a sound in the distance.

Police sirens.

The fire returned to her eyes and expression. "You called the cops on me?" Jordana growled.

"No, I called the cops on the shooter who tried to kill us," Nash clarified. "If that happens to be you —"

"Fuck off," Jordana snapped.

"The cops will want to speak to you," Nash pointed out, but he was talking to the air because Jordana was already turning the car around.

"Want me to go after her?" Slade asked.

"No." Nash didn't hesitate either. "The cops will do that. I don't want the gates open until I'm sure she's gone."

After what'd just happened to them, Caroline was relieved about that decision. But it did lead her to another of those big questions. Where would Nash and she go? They couldn't stay here because, like her place, it was now a crime scene where things would have to be searched and processed.

"I don't want to go to my mother's," Caroline threw out there as a preemptive strike.

Nash turned to her but then just as quickly turned back to the screen when Oz spoke. "A county deputy is at the gate, and the drone has detected something. Footage is loading to monitor now."

"The cop will have to wait," Nash told Oz. "I want to see what the footage is."

"Maybe the drone is following Jordana," Slade muttered.

But when the feed appeared, Caroline saw it wasn't of the driveway to Nash's house or the nearby road. Not of Jordana's car or the motorcycle in the ditch either. This was a small clearing in a heavily treed area.

And there was something dark in the center of it.

"Where is that?" Caroline asked.

Nash continued to study the feed. "I'm not sure. Oz, ask the drone operator for coordinates of the location of this image."

It didn't take long for Oz to obtain that info, and Nash pulled up a map on his phone. "It's a half mile from here and a quarter of a mile from the motorcycle. And it's not easy to access because of some deep gulleys and a mineral spring. The only way to get there is on foot."

The person operating the drone did some maneuvering, adjusting the camera and dropping down lower to zoom in on the dark object.

Caroline saw it then. Saw what it was.

A body.

Sweet heaven. It was a body.

The person was sprawled out and turned to the side so she couldn't tell who it was, but judging from the size, it was a man. One wearing all black and with a rifle next to him.

"I'm pretty sure that's the shooter," Nash commented.

"Yes," Caroline muttered, and she pinned her attention to the monitor as the drone did another adjustment, moving closer, going to the other side of the body. "Is that blood on the side of his shirt, or is it just wet?"

"It's blood." Nash touched the image pointing to the person's neck.

Where there was some kind of injury. A bullet hole maybe.

"Oz, instruct the drone operator to zoom in on the person's face," Nash said.

It took several moments, but the drone responded, dropping down until it was practically eye level with the body.

Oh, God.

CHAPTER THIRTEEN

———— ☆ ————

"The sonofabitch is dead," Caroline heard Nash mutter.

He sounded both shocked and comforted. A combination of emotions that Caroline completely understood. Because she was having a similar one as she stared at the dead man's face.

Bodie.

"He's dead," Caroline managed to say. "Bodie's really dead."

It certainly looked like it anyway, she tried to look at the scene with an objective eye. Hard to do when she was feeling a whole lot of relief right now. Relief that was short-lived though when Nash said something to shatter the moment.

"It's been set up to look like a suicide," Nash remarked.

Slade made a sound of agreement. "But the angle is off for the placement of the gun. Hard to kill yourself with a rifle and then have the gun and body land on the ground like that."

Caroline volleyed glances at both of them while the image was still frozen on the screen. "So, who would…"

She stopped because she immediately realized who could have done this.

"Jordana," she spat out. But she stopped again and shook her head. "Why kill him and then come here?"

"To try to establish an alibi," Nash was quick to say. "She could have been in those woods with him, and maybe Bodie said or did something to piss her off, and she shot him."

"Yes," Caroline muttered, and she recalled the way the woman had bashed her hand against the steering wheel when Nash had mentioned the *term of endearment* that Bodie had used in his text.

There had been a lot of rage there.

Rage that Jordana could have directed at her husband if Bodie had said something to his wife about that *darlin'* or his feelings for Caroline.

"Why don't you go ahead and get Caroline out of here?" Slade offered Nash. "Take her to my place on the lake so she can have a little time to deal with this before she has to face the cops and give a statement. I can let Ruby and the cops know what's going on as well."

Nash looked at her, and he couldn't nod fast enough. Probably because he could see there was no possible way she was ready to do an interview or be questioned. Added to that, the police would likely be focusing on getting to the body.

The body.

Those two words were really starting to sink in. Bodie was dead. He was no longer a threat.

But was Jordana?

Maybe with Bodie gone, she would give up on finishing what Bodie had started eighteen years ago. If Jordana was behind this, that is. It was still possible that Eddie or Leland was involved, though they personally couldn't have been the ones to fire those shots since they'd been at the police station at the time.

Caroline pushed thoughts of that aside when Nash picked up the bags from the console and turned to her. It felt as if she were on autopilot as Nash led her out of the van and to his vehicle. They got in his SUV and drove away just as the gates opened to let in the cops.

Or rather the *cop*.

It was a lone uniformed officer in the cruiser. He didn't try to stop them, which meant Slade had likely explained to him what was going on. Caroline was betting that Slade had also called for more officers, maybe someone from Maverick Ops, too, to go in and recover Bodie's body.

"Slade's lake house is only about fifteen miles away," Nash let her know.

Good. Not far. And it wouldn't take them long to get there at the speed that Nash was driving. Then, it occurred to her why he was going so fast. He probably thought she was on the verge of a total meltdown.

"I'm okay," she spelled out for him. "Maybe a little in shock, but I'm okay. I, uh...feel free," Caroline settled for saying.

But then she had to consider what this might be doing to Nash. After all, he'd just learned his brother was dead.

"Are you all right?" she asked.

He glanced at her. "I'm glad he's dead. Glad he's personally no longer a threat to you. But I'm still worried. Jordana needs to be found and questioned." Nash opened his mouth as if about to give Oz a command about that. Then, he stopped. "Slade will take care of it."

"Yes." She had no doubts about that. "Will Slade and Jericho be relieved, too, about Bodie?"

"They will be," Nash verified. "The three of us were never close to Bodie. The only one Bodie was close to our father."

"The abusive asshole," she muttered.

Nash nodded. "Yes, Bodie was his firstborn, and a son at that. Someone he could brag about to his asshole friends. I think he groomed Bodie to be the man he became." He paused a moment. "And I didn't do a damn thing to stop it."

And there it was. The guilt in his voice. Maybe the grief, too, for a sibling he hadn't been able to save.

Caroline touched his arm, rubbed gently. "I didn't save my father so I get what you're saying."

Nash frowned when he looked at her. "Your father died from cancer."

"He did, but guilt is a greedy SOB, and I kept thinking I could have done more. Maybe I could have noticed sooner that he wasn't his usual self. Maybe I could have insisted he go to the doctor right away. Part of me knows that isn't logical, that he would have died from that form of cancer anyway. But, like you, I wish I'd done more to try to save him."

"Done more," he repeated under his breath. "Thinking like that is what creates emotional baggage. And guilt. And regret. So much regret that I didn't stop Bodie from getting to you."

"Well, he's stopped now." And Caroline used that as a launching pad to go over some other things.

Things that might help Nash put his regret and guilt on the backburner.

"Maybe Bodie was stopped by his bride. Or by someone that her father could have hired. A nice setup for Leland," she added. "Get someone to kill the bane of his existence and make it look like a suicide."

He stayed quiet a moment, probably considering that. "Yes, and this way, Jordana won't disown her father for eliminating her beloved."

"A bonus," she decided. "So, that could mean Eddie wasn't involved in the attacks or Bodie's death."

Nash shrugged. "I'm not ruling him out just yet. He could have motive for wanting Bodie dead if he wants Jordana for himself. That sounds like a long shot," he tacked onto that. "But Eddie could be covering up his real feelings for Jordana, and he has plenty of ex-con friends who could have helped him."

Helped him by actually firing those shots both at her place and at Nash's. But now that Bodie was dead, did that mean Eddie would consider this vendetta to be over and done?

Caroline prayed so.

She tore her gaze from Nash when he slowed and took a turn. Not into some remote countryside either. This was the entrance to a gated subdivision, and beyond the gate and fence, she could see something that surprised her.

Houses.

Lots of them. Some cabin style, some more like mansions that'd been built on hills that surrounded the lake.

The large limestone sign announced that this was Pearl Bluff Estates, and there were indeed some pearly-colored bluffs in the distance. The view was definitely postcard-worthy.

"I guess I thought Slade would live somewhere more… secluded," she commented.

"You'd think, especially after being raised in a survivalists' compound. But unlike Jericho and me, Slade prefers living in a neighborhood. Though this doesn't quite qualify as that since it's mainly vacation homes. He splits time between here and his apartment on the Riverwalk in San Antonio."

Nash punched in a code when he reached the gate and then drove past four houses before he pulled into the driveway of a log cabin. Well, an upgraded cabin that also hit that postcard-worthy mark. It was two-story and with lots of windows and balconies.

"How secure is this place?" she had to ask, but then Caroline immediately waved that off. "It's very secure. Slade might prefer living around people, but he still works for Maverick Ops."

"It has all the right bells and whistles," Nash assured her, using another code to get into the garage.

She saw one of those bells and whistles right away. The door leading into the house had its own keypad, and Caroline thought it might be made of some kind of metal that'd been painted dark gray. If someone managed to break into the garage, they wouldn't have an easy time getting inside.

As with the gate and garage door, Nash entered yet another code, and the door slid open, reminding her of an entrance to a hotel. They stepped inside, not into a usual mudroom or small entry but into a massive equipment room that had shelf after shelf of weapons and gear.

The house seemed to spring to life. Lights flared on and music, too. Pink Floyd's *Another Brick in the Wall* began to pulse from...somewhere. Caroline couldn't spot any speakers.

They stepped into an open floorplan similar to Nash's place, but instead of the pasture, barn, and horses, Slade had a view of the lake. There were other differences as well. Slade had gone for vibrant colors. Cobalt blues, aqua, and yellow.

"Welcome, Nash and Caroline," a voice said, talking over the song. "Slade informed me you'd be arriving."

Caroline's forehead bunched up. "That sounds like Spock's voice from *Star Trek*."

"It is," Nash verified. "The song and the show were our mother's favorites. Well, favorites before we moved to Stronghold anyway. After that, we didn't have a TV, and my SOB of a father didn't allow her to listen to music. I think this is Slade's way of thumbing his nose at the bastard while still keeping part of her alive."

Yes, grief was very complex, and Slade had obviously worked out a way to deal with the loss.

"Caroline, as Slade instructed, the hot tub is ready for you to have a long soak," Spock added. "Nash, there's Oban in the liquor cabinet for you."

"Thanks," Nash muttered. "It's my favorite," he added to Caroline, and then he checked the time. "It's a little early for a drink, though."

She checked the time, too, and was shocked to see it was barely noon. Her body suddenly felt as if she'd been up for days. And in a way, she had been since she hadn't slept a wink the night before. Added to the lack of sleep was all that spent adrenaline from the attack.

"Where's the hot tub?" Caroline asked, glancing out onto the flagstone patio. It wasn't there.

Nash smiled and motioned for her to follow him. He led her past a large office and what appeared to be the main bedroom before he threw open double doors at the end of the hall.

And Caroline did some instant goggling.

"Wow," she muttered. "It looks like a gym and a spa combined."

"Yep."

He pointed to a sauna and a lap pool that ran against the entire back of the room. There was another wall of windows here with views of the lake and a side garden bursting with flowers. But the focal point of the room was the sunken hot tub in the center. It was the size of a half dozen regular tubs, and the jets churned and bubbled the steaming teal blue water.

Suddenly, every muscle in her body seemed to be aching to climb inside.

"Help yourself," Nash said. "There are some swimming clothes in the closet of the ensuite bath or you can take a soak commando since no one can see in through the windows. I'll grab you a glass of wine."

While that sounded wonderful, Caroline thought of something else that would work a whole lot better than wine.

A kiss.

So, that's what she did. She took hold of his hand, pulling him to her and pressing her mouth to his. He stiffened a little, maybe because he was well aware that the kiss could end up being the start of a whole lot more.

And that's what she was hoping.

It seemed to hit her hard and fast. The realization that while a soak in the hot tub and wine would indeed be nice, it wouldn't fix what Nash could do just by being with her.

"We're playing with fire," he muttered with his mouth against her.

"Yes, we are. Very hot fire." She kissed him again, deepening it this time, and his taste glided through her.

The kiss continued and got even deeper. The heat came. The hunger, too. Hunger for Nash, and she could feel he was having the same reaction to her. That's why she was surprised when he eased back.

"You're exhausted," he said, lifting a finger. "You're probably still in shock." A second finger went up as he continued his tally of why he should be leaving her alone. "You need to relax and process what's happened." A third finger went up. "And after a soak and some wine, you need sleep."

"All true," she admitted, "but I'm not as exhausted as I was just a few minutes ago." She moved closer, brushing her body against his. "In fact, I'm more than a little revved up."

The corner of his mouth lifted in a smile. Then, he groaned. "This feels like taking advantage of you."

"Always the hero," she muttered. "So, let me take advantage of you. Let me finish what we started at that party."

Even with that blatant invitation, she thought he might decline and do the hero thing by giving her some time alone. Time that she didn't want. So, she kissed him again, this time pressing herself against him.

He made a sound, sort of a groan-grunt combo, and the rest of his resolve seemed to snap because Nash hooked his arm around her waist and hauled her to him. All those muscles made it easy for him to do the maneuver.

She might have cheered in triumph if his mouth hadn't claimed hers. Now, this was a kiss. A scalding, scorching kiss that promised so much more to come.

And more came.

He slid his mouth and tongue down to her neck. Then, to the front of her shirt. Her body reacted all right, and this time the heat didn't just glide, it roared through her. Parts of her started to make demands. Demands that Nash seemed well on the way to fulfilling when he took those torturous kisses to the front of her shirt.

To her breasts.

Caroline got so caught up in the pleasure of the moment. Caught in the fantasy of being with Nash like this. That she forgot something major.

Something that she got an instant reminder of when Nash lifted her shirt.

She stepped back, and with her breath gusting, she stared at him. "The scars," she managed to say.

"I, uh, don't want you to see them again."

"Because you think it'll make me want you less?" he asked.

He closed the distance between them and kissed her with his breath. No mouth-to-mouth contact. Just the breath that carried his scent, his taste, and some kind of erotic pull that made her want to jump him right then, right there.

"Trust me," he said, his voice a slow, easy drawl that was his own form of foreplay. "Wanting you less isn't an option for me."

She wanted to argue. Caroline wanted to tell him that he could be wrong. That he might change his mind when he saw, and touched, the scars.

But she wanted him more than either of those other things.

So, she stepped toward him, straight into his waiting arms. Nash didn't make her wait though for anything else. He picked up where he'd left off with the kisses, trailing from her mouth, to her neck, to the front of her shirt. Then, he lifted it, shoving down her bra and giving her some well-placed kisses that had her drowning in pleasure.

And falling.

Except, no. Not falling.

He was lowering her to the smooth stone rim of the hot tub where he gently placed her on her back. The kisses continued, and he appeared to be on a sensual journey to explore every part of her body because he kissed her stomach next, circling her naval with his tongue.

She had a fleeting thought of his mouth on her scars. Just fleeting though. Hard to think of scars when he was doling out such sweet torture.

Along with getting her naked.

Nash pulled off her top. Her bra. She felt the warm, misty air settle on her skin as he exposed more and more of her by taking off her shoes and shimmying her jeans down her legs.

Her panties, too.

Before she could protest that she was now naked and he wasn't, he gave her a kiss that rendered her speechless. Heck, it nearly caused her to climax. Because he kissed her between her legs, right in her center.

She closed her eyes, arching her back and accepting everything he was giving her. For a couple of seconds anyway. When she felt that climax about to roll through her, Caroline put the pause button on her pleasure and did a role reversal.

Nash probably could have stopped her from moving, from maneuvering him so that he was lying on the floor and she was on top of him. He didn't because she didn't give him a chance. She kissed him, hard and deep, as he'd done to her, and she started that whole getting him naked part.

And what an adventure that was.

She got off his shoulder holster and the rest of his weapons, including his phone. Then, his shirt. She might have gone straight for his jeans, but mercy, she had to take a moment to admire the view. The man was built.

"Good grief," she muttered. "No one has a right to look this good."

He smiled. "I feel the same way about you."

That was probably BS, but she didn't give that much thought. Correction—she *couldn't* give it much thought. That's because she was focused on something that felt much more urgent.

Kissing her way down all those toned and tanned muscles.

She kissed her way down to the zipper of his jeans. Because she got so caught up in the sensations of having her mouth on his body, she didn't feel herself getting too close to the edge.

Not a metaphor for an orgasm either.

But the edge of the hot tub.

Nash and she rolled in, sinking straight into the steamy water.

After she gasped from the shock of it, she laughed. So did he. But their bodies quickly adjusted to the change of location, and they kissed again. And again. Nash added some touching, too, by cupping her butt and pressing her center against his erection.

Of course, that particular part of him was still covered by his jeans, so she did something about that. It wasn't easy though, not when the kissing took on a fresh urgency. Not when her body was begging for her to get him naked.

Nash helped with that last part. He managed to get out of his jeans and boxers. But just as important, he managed something else. He went through his now-soaked wallet and came up with a condom.

Caroline silently cursed for not remembering safe sex, but soon, she forgot all about the near lapse. That's because Nash jumped straight back to the kissing. To the touching. All the while he managed to get on the condom. It was very effective multitasking.

He anchored her against the side of the hot tub, right on a jet that was giving her some amazing sensations on her backside, while Nash gave her even more amazing sensations on her front.

By hooking her legs around his waist and pushing into her.

The fresh wave of pleasure came fast, filling her. Spreading through her. She got lost in it. Got lost in Nash.

Thankfully, he didn't treat her like glass. There was gentleness but a hard urgency, too, that told her he needed her as much as she needed him. The thrusts inside her became harder, faster, deeper.

And each one took her closer and closer to that peak.

She wanted to hang on. Wanted to make this last. But she couldn't. Nash saw to that. He quickened the pace, and then he claimed her mouth with his just as the climax rippled through her.

Pleasure. So much pleasure. No thoughts, no words. Just the sensation of being taken by a man who knew exactly how to make her fly.

She flew all right.

And once Nash had stretched out every last moment of her climax, he flew right along with her.

CHAPTER FOURTEEN

———— ☆ ————

Nash read through the report he'd just gotten while he kept an eye on Caroline. Not that she was going anywhere. She was exactly where she'd been for the past half hour since they'd gotten out of the hot tub.

Asleep on the sofa.

He'd been worried that sex might be too much for her, that she could have regrets and doubts, but it seemed to have the opposite effect. She'd dressed, kissed him some more, and snuggled up on the sofa while waiting for any updates. Before the first update had come through, she'd been sound asleep, and Nash was hoping she'd stay that way for a while.

Now, he was the one wide awake and dealing with the doubts. No regrets though about having sex with Caroline. Being with her had seemed, well, a necessity rather than for mere pleasure. The pleasure had certainly been there though, and it hadn't sated his need for her. Just the opposite. He wanted her all over again.

That led him to the big question that kept flashing in his mind.

What was next for them?

Or was there even a next?

One-time sex didn't mean there had to be a next. But he knew there would be…something. Dates, maybe? A relationship? More?

It troubled him that he wanted more. That she might not need the same. If so, then he couldn't press for anything other than what she could give him. That didn't mean it wouldn't hurt like hell if she walked away.

But he couldn't blame her if she did.

It was one thing to say he didn't remind her of Bodie, of the attack. It was an entirely different thing to try to cope with on a daily basis.

With that dismal possibility joining the flashing question in his head, he forced his attention back on the two updates he'd gotten. The first was from Slade, and the second was from Ruby.

Slade had joined the team of county cops, the medical examiner, and two CSIs who were finally on their way to that clearing where they'd seen the body. Finally, because it'd taken some time for the team to be assembled. Slade expected to be able to give him more info once they'd reached the site on foot.

Nash moved onto Ruby's report and immediately frowned when he read the first line.

Jordana was still missing, and Ruby was concerned as to what the woman would do next. He figured that concern was warranted. If Jordana had indeed killed Bodie, then she might be on the run to escape arrest. Might even already be out of the country.

But Jordana could also have something else in mind.

Like coming after Caroline.

Since that possibility had already occurred to Nash, it was the reason he had Slade's security system on full operation. Because it might not just be Jordana they had to be concerned about but also Eddie. Or even someone else that Jordana had hired to help her.

Also, according to Ruby's report, neither Eddie nor Leland was still at the police station. Eddie because his lawyer had managed to reschedule the remainder of the interview and Leland because there'd been no grounds to hold him after he'd given his statement. That meant Eddie could be out to settle an old score for Bodie. No better way to do that than to try to kill Caroline.

At least Nash didn't think they had to be concerned about Leland. No old scores for him to settle.

However, Nash immediately rethought that.

Leland wouldn't try to deal with Bodie's unfinished business with Caroline, but the man might be willing to go to any lengths to protect his daughter. That could include silencing anyone who could implicate her in Bodie's death.

Including Caroline and him.

After all, they had seen her reaction when she'd driven up to his gate, and if Jordana went running to Daddy to whine about witnesses who might be able to point the finger at her, then Nash could see Leland going into the fixer mode.

So, Leland was staying on the watch list.

His phone vibrated a split-second before something else flashed on the desk monitor, and Nash saw the alert.

Incoming drone feed.

Normally, Spock or Oz would have verbally alerted him to something like that, but he'd put both on silent mode so it wouldn't wake Caroline.

Nash watched the footage as the drone picked up the movement of four men and two women who were snaking their way through a trail in the woods. Slade and two uniformed county cops were in the lead, with the two CSIs behind them. Nash figured the other man was the medical examiner.

There were enough thick clusters of trees that the drone lost sight of them for several moments before they reappeared again. Judging from the coordinates the drone showed, they'd soon be in the clearing. And Slade would have to deal with seeing Bodie's body.

Nash didn't think Slade would experience any kind of grief or sadness over the *loss*. Just the opposite. Still, it would be a sucker punch to see their brother lying on the ground.

Behind him, he heard Caroline stir, and he hoped she'd go back to sleep. Because it would be a sucker punch for her, too, to see her now-dead attacker. But no such luck. He turned when Caroline sat up and yawned.

"I crashed," she muttered, stretching.

She looked at him. Smiled. But the smile didn't last when she spotted what was on the screen.

"Did anything happen while I was out?" she blurted, practically springing off the sofa and hurrying toward him. She kept her attention pinned to the screen.

"No sign of Jordana, and that's about it," he summarized. "Slade had to wait for the other responders and the ME to arrive before they could go out to the body, so that's why there was a delay."

She pulled over a chair, positioning it right next to his, and she leaned over, giving him a quick, almost absent kiss. He looked at her, causing her gaze to shift from the screen to him. She smiled again. Then, she kissed him for real.

Oh, that felt damn good having her mouth on his, and he hated that the timing sucked for a round two. Later, maybe, especially since they might have to stay here for a while until both his and her places had been processed.

His phone vibrated again, and a text from Slade popped up on the bottom of the drone feed. "Arrived in the clearing," Caroline read aloud.

That got their attention back on the screen, and they had the aerial view of the team walking toward the body. Slowly. All of them, even the ME, were checking the ground to make sure they didn't step on anything that might be evidence. That would especially be needed if it turned out that this wasn't death by suicide.

Which Nash was certain it wasn't.

He was betting this was murder.

One of the cops pointed to something and then pulled a small yellow flag from his pocket to mark the spot. According to the next text that Slade sent, it was several shoeprints in some mud.

The drone dropped down, going closer to the body as Slade and the cops approached. Slade stayed back a little, recording the scene on his phone. Probably since it would give him a different view than the drone.

A cop went to one side of the body, crouching down to look at Bodie's face. The second went to the other, his attention focused on the neck wound. And while Nash couldn't hear what they weren't saying, he did see something that sent a spike of alarm through him.

One of the cops stood abruptly and appeared to be cursing.

Slade and the other cop moved in, going to the side where they could see Bodie's face. That spike of alarm got even harder and bigger when Slade's expression turned to ice, and he pressed something on his phone.

Moments later Nash's phone buzzed not with a text but rather a call from Slade.

Hell.

Something was definitely wrong.

"What happened?" Nash couldn't ask fast enough.

Slade wasn't so quick to answer, though, and Nash watched him draw in a long breath. "It's not Bodie."

Nash shook his head.

Caroline made a soft gasping sound.

"But we saw him on the feed," Caroline insisted. "It has to be him. He has to be dead."

"It's not him," Slade said, his voice as strained as his expression. "I don't know who the hell he is, but he's wearing a mask of sorts." He paused, seemed to struggle with what he added next. "It's a picture of Bodie taped to the dead man's face."

CHAPTER FIFTEEN

———— ☆ ————

"This is hell," Caroline heard herself mutter. "I'm in hell."

She knew that she sounded on the verge of a full-blown panic attack. And she hated to worry Nash like that.

Hated to feel like this.

But she couldn't stop herself from repeating that *I'm in hell* over and over while she pressed her hands to the sides of her head and tried to wrap her mind around what she'd just learned.

That Bodie wasn't dead.

She'd been so relieved when she'd thought it was over. When she'd been certain that he'd never be able to hurt her or anyone else again. So relieved that she'd felt…alive. So whole. She hadn't felt like a victim.

But now, all those old feelings had returned with a vengeance and were like a swamp around her. Hot and dirty, reeking of dark, dangerous things ready to rip her to pieces.

Yeah, that panic attack was coming, all right.

"Sit," she heard Nash say, and that's when she realized she had fisted her hands in her hair and was pacing. Not a slow movement either. She was practically running around the room.

Nash gently took her by the hand and led her back to the sofa. She sat because she wasn't sure her legs could even support her at the moment. She wasn't sure of anything except this rising dread that was coming on so fast that it was impossible to tamp it down.

"So, where is he?" she managed to ask. "If that's not his body, then where's Bodie?"

"To be determined," Slade said.

Oh, God.

That was *not* what she wanted to hear. She needed him caught. She needed him dead.

Caroline tried to rein in her fears. Tried to focus. Or move. Or do anything that would help her fight this. But at the moment, it didn't feel as if this was a fight she could win.

She had to change that.

She couldn't let Bodie beat her. Not after she'd come so far in recovering from what he'd done to her.

Caroline forced her attention back to the drone feed, where she could now see Slade moving away from the body. He was no doubt hurrying to his vehicle so he could then go looking for Bodie. She prayed Slade or someone else would find him right away.

Maybe Bodie had stayed near the body, and Slade would spot him. But she immediately had to rethink that. There'd be no reason for Bodie to do that. In fact, there was an even bigger reason for him to be far, far away from the body.

So he couldn't be caught.

If he'd simply wanted to see the reactions of the responders, then he could have set up a camera. And he might have done just that. He could be watching right now, just as she was.

"Is everything secure there?" Slade asked.

"It is," Nash verified. "I'll contact Ruby and get a team out—"

"No, I'll contact Ruby," Slade interrupted. "You take care of Caroline. How is she... Never mind. Stupid assed question. I already know how she is. She's shaken to the core."

Yeah. She was, and Caroline figured that applied to all three of them and soon to Ruby as well since she'd been worried for her daughter's safety.

"Try to track down Jordana, Eddie, and Leland," Slade advised. "Because either they're targets or possible accomplices."

Nash muttered a quick agreement and ended the call, immediately turning back toward her. "I want you to use the second computer on Slade's desk," he instructed, his words surprisingly calm. That calmness probably didn't extend beneath the surface, though. "Spock will help you access the feed from traffic cameras and show you how to

153

apply facial recognition."

Caroline nearly asked him if this was busy work, something to keep her mind off Bodie being alive. But even if it was a task merely meant to stop her from panicking, it might help. It would especially help if she managed to spot Jordana, Leland or Eddie because Bodie might be near one of them.

Or after them.

Because Slade was right about them being potential targets.

"My guess is Bodie will try to kill Leland," Nash went on, taking the words right out of her mouth.

He took hold of her arm and led her to the desk. He then eased her into the chair and moved a laptop in front of her.

"You mean because Jordana would then inherit everything, and then Bodie could kill her?" she asked.

"Exactly. Because I'm not buying that he's in love with her."

Nash picked up the laptop he'd been on earlier for the reports and moved both it and a chair next to her. She was glad he'd done that. Caroline wanted him close right now. Needed to draw some of his strength so she could focus.

"And Eddie?" Nash went on. "Bodie could plan to kill him, too. He set up that body for a reason. Probably to buy him some time. Maybe to get his targets to relax a bit and come out in the open."

Caroline had to suppress a shiver at that

thought. Bodie could have been waiting for them on the road when they drove here. Then again, maybe he'd been waiting in the other direction, which is the way they would have gone had she decided to stay with her mother. Perhaps Bodie decided he'd have a fifty-fifty chance of catching them, and if that was the case, it pleased her that he'd been wrong.

"Spock, load the live feed for any traffic cameras within a twenty-mile radius of Caroline's house, mine, and here. Ruby's too," he added. "Put the feed on both the wall monitor and laptop number two."

Caroline glanced at him, her eyebrow now raised. "For Bodie to cover all those places, he'd need help. More help than just Jordana."

"He would," Nash agreed, "but we don't know if he's getting assistance from someone like Eddie. Maybe another felon who thinks of him as fondly as Eddie does. Ruby did a report on all of Bodie's recent visitors, and a couple of names popped of men who'd served time with Bodie before their releases. She's trying to track them down."

Good. Caroline wanted all angles covered. Anything that would lead them back to Bodie.

The traffic feed loaded on the screens. Not from just one camera but from four. The images were in a split view on the laptop, and Caroline started pouring through them. She'd never even seen footage from a traffic camera, but she could spot the vehicles in range of the lens.

"Focus on looking at the faces in the vehicles," Nash told her. "Since we don't know what any of them will be driving."

True. So, that's what she did, and the sea of faces sped by. She soon realized this was like finding a needle in a fast-moving haystack.

"I could easily miss one of them," she muttered.

He made a sound of agreement. "You could, but the facial recognition program is engaged, and it's checking, too."

Caroline didn't exactly relax after hearing that. Relaxing wasn't going to happen until Bodie was found. But at least it didn't feel as if spotting him was solely on Nash's and her shoulders. Plenty of cops were looking for him. Leland and Jordana would be, too. But the traffic feed and facial recognition could cover a lot of ground.

Nash's phone vibrated, and he muttered something about needing to turn the ringer back on. He did. Then, he frowned when he looked at the caller ID.

"It's from the county sheriff's office," he relayed to her, and he answered the call on speaker.

"Mr. McKenna, I'm Drew Gomez, a dispatcher for the county, and someone is trying to call you. Eddie Mulcrone. He says it's important. Should I put the call through?"

"Yes," Nash insisted while he typed in something on his keyboard. "He might know where Bodie is," he added to Caroline.

Seconds later, Eddie's frantic voice poured

through the house. "McKenna, it's me, Eddie. I just heard that Bodie tried to fake his death. That's he alive."

"Where did you hear that?" Nash asked.

Eddie wasn't so fast with a response that time. "Jordana. She called me, and it's a big-assed understatement to say she's upset. Bodie's not answering her calls, and she thinks he might have found out about that picture of the two of us kissing." He whispered that last part.

"And you think Bodie will now come after you and kill you," Nash commented.

"Hell, yeah, that's what I think," Eddie snapped. "And he will. Your brother can be very possessive."

A burst of air left Caroline's mouth. A laugh but not from humor. Definitely not humor. But she knew plenty about Bodie's *possessive* streak.

"Where's Jordana?" Nash asked, obviously shifting the conversation a little.

"I have no idea. That's the truth," Eddie insisted when Nash huffed. "She's not going to tell me something like that. She doesn't trust me. She thinks I'd throw her under a bus with Bodie by trying to save my own skin."

"And you would," Nash said. It wasn't a question.

"Hey, you're trying to save Caroline's fine ass so I'm not going to apologize for wanting to save mine." He paused a heartbeat. "I just don't want you ratting me out to Bodie. That kiss with Jordana meant nothing, and I don't want to die because of it."

Eddie ended the call, and Nash quickly checked something on his laptop screen. He dropped some f-bombs under his breath. "Eddie was using a burner. No immediate trace available on his location."

She hadn't even known he'd tried to do a trace, and she was sorry it'd failed. Eddie had made it seem as if he was scared, but that could have all been an act. Caroline couldn't understand why

Though, since there was no way Nash or she would trust the man enough to give him any useful info. They sure as heck weren't going to cover for him.

Before Nash had even set his phone aside, it rang, and she saw him visibly tense. His shoulders went back, and his jaw tightened. She had a similar reaction when he showed her what was on the screen.

Unknown Caller.

She suddenly didn't have the breath to urge him to answer it. But she knew in her gut who this was.

And she was right.

Nash took the call on speaker but didn't issue a greeting. He just waited for the caller to speak.

"Hey, darlin'," Bodie said. "Surprised to hear from me? I mean, since you thought I was dead and all."

Caroline took a moment. Regained her breath and glanced at Nash to let him know that she was going to respond. Hard to do, but Nash was trying to trace the call, and this time, they might get lucky.

"Yes, I did think you were dead," she was finally able to say. Thank heaven her voice hadn't cracked, and she sounded a hell of a lot stronger than she felt. "Why did you fake your death?"

"Oh, to buy me some time." His dismissive tone set her teeth on edge. "Cops don't look for dead men."

"No, but they will now," she was quick to assure him. "They know you murdered someone else and plastered a mask of yourself on him. So, no attempted charges this time around. It'll be a full-blown first-degree murder conviction. Maybe you'll even get a needle in the arm to end your worthless life."

Bodie laughed. "Oh, boo fuckin' hoo. Don't feel sorry for the dead guy. He was a first-class dick. Barney Coltrain."

Nash quickly put in a search on the name while Bodie continued his gloating and gushing.

"Barney had a rap sheet, well, as long as the beautiful scars on your body. I did a service to humanity by eliminating him. You can thank me since the asshole nearly killed you."

"So, he's the one who fired the shots at me?" she asked.

"Hell, yeah, it was him," Bodie verified. "I only wanted him to flush you out with that tear gas shit, and he starts blasting away like some special ops sniper." He paused. "He didn't hurt you, did he, darlin'?"

Caroline tried to make her voice sound as flippant as his. "No. There's not a scratch on me."

"Good. Because I'm the only one who has a right to put marks on you, not asshole convicts who don't follow orders." The anger dripped from those last few words. Bodie clearly didn't like being crossed or challenged.

Or dumped.

"What do you want, Bodie?" she demanded.

"Oh, I want so very much, Caroline," he said, shifting to a sappy sweet tone that turned her stomach. Then again, everything about the man caused her to have that reaction. "So very, very much. But let's start with a simple visit. You come to me, and you do it now."

Caroline had an *Oh, God* moment of near panic before she remembered Bodie wasn't right there in the room with her. He wasn't standing behind her with a skinning knife, and he didn't have control over her.

"And why would I do that?" she asked. "Why would I come to you?"

"Because of her," Bodie readily answered. The sappiness went up a significant notch. "All because of her."

"Who?" she snapped.

"Your mama, that's who." Bodie laughed long and hard. "I got her, Caroline. I have Ruby."

CHAPTER
SIXTEEN

———— ☆ ————

Nash silently cursed every word of profanity that he knew. And he forced the muscles in his body to unclench. He needed to stay level. Needed to think.

Because he didn't believe Bodie was lying about having Ruby.

On some off chance that he was, Nash used the landline on the desk to try to call his boss. And it went straight to voicemail.

Hell.

Bodie had her all right. With everything going on, Ruby would have answered if she had been able to do it.

Dreading what he would see, he looked at Caroline. She was way too pale and understandably shaking. But he saw some fight in her, too. Some anger.

Good.

Nash might have to tap into that anger to keep her strong for what they were about to face. And what they were about to face would be bad. The stuff of nightmares for Caroline.

"Still there, darlin'?" Bodie asked in a taunt. "Hope the cat didn't get your tongue."

"It didn't," Caroline snapped, and Nash saw another burst of anger. "Where's my mother?"

"Right here with me," Bodie supplied. "And now I'm going to have her say something. A proof of life kind of deal since I figured that's something you'd press for. What would you like for her to say so I can have her repeat it?"

Caroline looked at Nash, and he jotted down a question. "Where is Bodie holding you?" she read.

Moments later, he heard Ruby's voice. "Where is Bodie holding you," she repeated.

There was the sound of some kind of movement, and Nash got the sense that Ruby had been about to add something else, but Bodie had silenced her. He didn't want to think of *how* Bodie would have accomplished that. Ruby wasn't an easy person to intimidate.

Or to capture.

"How did Bodie get to you?" Nash asked.

"Ah, my brother," Bodie said as if that called for some kind of celebration. "Of course, I knew you were there. Joined at the hip with Caroline, aren't you? I'm guessing you don't mind getting my leftovers."

Shit. That did it. This time it was more than anger that crossed Caroline's face. It was pure, raging fury.

"You limp dick loser," Caroline spat out. "You

never had me, so I'm not your leftovers."

Bodie laughed, but, oh, there was a dangerous edge to it. He did not like being dressed down by anyone, not even his obsession.

Nash was glad that Caroline had managed to get in that dig, but this was a lethal game, and at the moment, Bodie had the advantage.

Because he had Ruby.

"So, how do you see this playing out, *brother*?" Nash snarled because, hey, he was dealing with his own rage for this sonofabitch.

"I see it playing out with Caroline exchanging herself for her mother," Bodie answered without a heartbeat of hesitation.

There was some more movement on the other end of the line, and Nash wondered if once again, Ruby had tried to get in her own two cents worth. No way would Ruby want Caroline to make an exchange like that. But then, Caroline wouldn't just stand by and let her mother be killed in her place.

Damn it all to hell.

That meant this was the ultimate rock and a hard place.

Because Nash didn't intend to let either Caroline or Ruby die.

"Where is this exchange supposed to happen?" Nash asked while he fired off a message to Slade to let him know what was going on. Slade should be able to tap into Spock and listen to the rest of the conversation for himself.

"So very close," Bodie answered. "I made it convenient for you. All you have to do is come to the security gate. You know the one. You would have driven through it to take Caroline into Slade's house."

Yeah, that was close. Damn close. And risky since it was daylight.

Nash went with a deflection ploy. One that wouldn't work, but he needed time for Slade to respond. "What makes you think we're at the lake house?"

"Oh, don't bullshit a bullshitter, Nash. My beautiful but often clueless bride helped with that before I even got out of that hellhole prison where Caroline had me locked away. Weeks ago, Jordana used some of her money to set up little bitty cameras every damn where. If there was a possibility that Caroline would be in or around a place, then it's got a camera."

Yeah, Nash could see Jordana doing that if Bodie asked her to do it. Anything for her husband, but she couldn't have been pleased about her man giving so much attention to another woman.

"Jordana is a good obedient lapdog," Bodie went on. "And she didn't skimp on quality for the cameras. She got good ones with crystal clear feed so I could see Caroline's face wherever she was coming or going. Or running scared. I liked looking at those."

Nash did more cursing and not just because Bodie was being a prime asshole with all this goading. He cursed because it meant Bodie had been planning this for a while. And apparently, planning it well. Still, it was very risky to try to go after Caroline like this.

And that meant Bodie had likely taken other precautions.

For one thing, Bodie probably wasn't alone with Ruby right now. Jordana could be nearby. Or maybe one of his thug friends. Nash was betting the one doing the assisting was poised and ready to shoot.

Not at Caroline.

But at him.

Bodie would know he'd be going with her and would want to eliminate the threat. Then, he could try to kill both Caroline and Ruby.

Try.

Because neither woman was going to make this easy for him. Still, Bodie could use them to his advantage. While Ruby and Caroline were trying to save each other, he could strike then. And he might win.

Damn it.

Bodie could maybe make this work.

"Here's the deal," Bodie went on. "Caroline has to come right now. I don't want to give Slade or somebody else time to get here. Be at the gate in five minutes, or I start stabbing holes in Caroline's mommy."

With that, the taunting and goading were apparently over because Bodie ended the call.

Caroline practically jumped out of the chair. "We can use some of Slade's equipment," she said right off the bat.

Nash was already heading to the supply room, and he handed her a Kevlar vest. "Remember, this doesn't stop a head shot. This might."

He handed her a helmet. Not the bulky kind but an experimental model that one of Ruby's techs had designed. It was lightweight and didn't cut down on visibility nearly as much as the regular ones.

"You're wearing one, too," she insisted. "Of course, Bodie didn't say you had to come with me..." She stopped when she obviously noticed his quick glare. "But you're going." She stopped again. "Thank you for that. But don't get killed, okay? Just don't get killed."

"Right back at you."

And because he thought they both needed it, he kissed her. Nothing long and deep since those minutes were ticking away. But he made the kiss count.

Then, he hoped it wouldn't be their last.

"Grab whatever weapon you think you can use," he instructed when he eased away from her.

She did. Caroline stuffed a Sig Sauer in the back waist of her jeans and took a Glock that she gripped in her hand.

"I have my knife," she said, tapping the holder on the outside of her boot. "I'm betting Bodie will have one, too."

Bodie would. No doubts about that. The asshole was going to try to recreate the attack from eighteen years ago.

Nash grabbed another Glock to go with his primary and backup guns, and he shoved both a smoke bomb and a tear gas canister into his pockets. Then, he checked the time.

Three minutes.

They went to his SUV just as Nash's phone rang. "Slade," he told her, and he took the call while he drove out of the garage.

"What's going on?" Slade immediately asked.

"Bodie has Ruby. He's at the gate of your lake house, and Caroline and I are heading there now."

"Wait for me," Slade insisted.

"Can't," Nash let him know. "Bodie gave us five minutes, and we have just enough time to make it."

Which had no doubt been a key component in this plan. Bodie hadn't wanted them to be able to come up with a way to stop this.

Slade cursed. "I'm on the way. I'll be there in ten."

Nash knew that wouldn't be soon enough. Well, not unless they could stall Bodie. But Bodie would no doubt be anticipating just that and would want to act before help arrived.

He ended the call with Slade and drove to the gate, a trip that seemed to fly by at lightning speed. But it'd eaten up all but ninety seconds of the deadline. Not enough time for him to do much, but he gave Caroline one critical instruction.

"If shots are fired, get down," he told her.

"You'll do the same?" she asked.

He considered lying but decided she wouldn't believe it anyway. "No. I'll return fire, but I'll need you to get down so I don't have to worry about watching you and whoever's shooting at me."

Spelling that out was slathering her with guilt. But maybe it would work to keep her alive. Of course, even if she did get down, that wasn't going to stop him from worrying about her. Down didn't mean she'd have adequate cover to stop her from being shot.

She sighed but didn't argue. No time for that either. The moment he stopped, he used the code to open the gate. They got out and started toward a showdown that was eighteen years in the making.

Nash kept slightly ahead of Caroline, and he fired glances around them, looking for a shooter. Looking for Bodie and Ruby, too.

He didn't see either of them.

He also didn't hear anything. It wasn't as quiet as a tomb but close enough, what with no birds chirping, wind blowing or people talking. Then again, it was a Wednesday, and most residents probably didn't come here until the weekend.

Nash motioned for Caroline to follow him to the side of the gate, where there was a metal box to manually key in codes. The wrought iron fence next to it also had thick pylons that he hoped would prevent Caroline and him from being shot from behind. For that to happen though, the shooter would have had to get inside the neighborhood.

A possibility.

But Nash figured there was an easier hiding place. He put his money on either the eight-foot-high limestone sign for the neighborhood or one of the deep ditches on the sides of the private road. There were some trees, but they weren't nearly tall or thick enough for a sniper to perch in one and send a hail of bullets their way.

"Time's up," he heard Bodie say.

His brother stepped out from behind the limestone sign, and he had Ruby positioned in front of him in a chokehold. Bodie had used duct tape on both her wrists and ankles.

But she was alive.

For now.

However, Bodie had the tip of a skinning knife pressed to her neck, no doubt right on the carotid artery. One jab and Ruby would bleed out long before the EMTs could arrive.

Behind him, Nash felt Caroline move, and for a second he thought she might bolt out to get to her mother. She didn't. She stayed put, but Nash could hear her now labored breathing.

"Ah, you came dressed up just for me," Bodie purred. "All that gear. But, you know, darlin', there are still plenty of places to put a knife." He laughed. "Then again, you have personal experience with that, don't you?"

Nash skipped asking Ruby if she was all right.

Clearly, she wasn't. So, he went with another question. "How did Bodie get to you?" And while she answered, Nash would take the time to assess if he had a clean shot to end Bodie's miserable life.

It wasn't Ruby who answered though. But rather Bodie.

"In the parking lot of the county sheriff's office," Bodie spelled out. "Ruby must not have thought I'd be ballsy enough to hang out there, what with all those badges around. But since being ballsy is my forte, I aimed a gun at her before she could draw hers. Then, I asked her something. Something real important. I said: *Are you willing to die to save your baby girl?*"

"Hell," he heard Caroline mutter.

That was very mild profanity compared to what Nash spat out.

"FYI," Bodie went on. "She told me yes, she'd be willing to die if I left Caroline alone. I swore to her on my own mama's grave that I would, that it'd be enough for me to have Caroline suffering and grieving over her mother's death." He paused. Grinned. "But, of course, I lied. Suffering and grieving aren't enough." Bodie licked Ruby's cheek, causing her to grimace. "Never trust a convicted felon."

"I didn't trust you," Ruby said. "I just hoped Caroline wouldn't come, that she'd see it for the trap that it was."

"It's not a trap unless it works," Nash countered, and he aimed a hard stare at Bodie. "Are you here to talk us to death? To bore us with your bullshit? Which, by the way, makes you sound like... I'll borrow a phrase from Caroline. A limp dick loser."

Maybe that would goad Bodie into moving just enough for that kill shot. Something that at the moment Nash didn't have.

Bodie glared at him. But didn't move.

"Sorry to bore you," Bodie growled. "However, it's not you that I want dead. I want the suffering and grief for you as a survivor to this payback mission. Same for Ruby, too. The only person who needs to die today is Caroline." He shifted his attention to her. "So, are you woman enough to take what's coming to you, or are you going to risk the lives of your lover boy and your mama?"

"I'm woman enough," Caroline verified with absolutely no hesitation. "By the way, a wise man once told me, 'Don't bring a knife to a gunfight.'"

Amused or at least pretending to be anyway, Bodie chuckled. "This isn't a gunfight."

"You're wrong about that," Caroline said like a challenge.

And she stepped to Nash's side, causing him to do a whole lot of silent cursing. He was ready to jump in front of her if she tried to take another step. But she didn't get the chance.

The sound of the approaching car had Bodie quickly ducking back behind the sign.

Obviously, this visitor wasn't part of his plan, and Nash knew it was way too soon for Slade to arrive.

And he was right.

It wasn't Slade.

The black Jaguar sped toward them, skidding to a stop. Seconds later, the driver barreled out. He didn't have a lawyer with him today. No bodyguard driver either. He was alone and clearly spoiling for a fight.

Leland.

CHAPTER SEVENTEEN

──────── ☆ ────────

"Where the hell is he?" Leland shouted the moment he was out of his car. "Where is that worthless scumbag who married my daughter?"

Judging from those questions, Leland had expected to find Bodie here. Why? Caroline was about to demand that info, but Bodie stepped out from behind the sign. He still had her mother in a chokehold.

She tried not to look directly into her mother's eyes. This ordeal was already impossible, but seeing the fear would only add another level to it. Not for fear for herself, either.

But for Caroline.

Her mother would do anything to keep her from dying, even if it meant letting Bodie kill her where she stood.

Caroline also saw Bodie lean his head slightly to the left, probably not enough to give Nash a clean shot, though. Bodie murmured something into a small communicator clipped to his collar.

So, he wasn't working alone.

Then again, she hadn't thought he would do this solo. He'd want to have someone to take care of Nash while he murdered her. But Caroline was going to do everything possible to make sure that didn't happen.

While Bodie's attention was on Leland, she glanced around, looking for Bodie's accomplice. She didn't spot anything or anyone suspicious, but there were several large boats in docks, and it was possible that someone was on one of them. Someone with a long-range rifle.

Jordana maybe?

"You stupid sonofabitch," Leland barked, aiming the insult at Bodie. "Do you know what'll happen if you kill Ruby Maverick?" He didn't wait for Bodie to respond. "You'll bring down the entire Maverick Ops' team on your stupid head, that's what. The entire team," he shouted.

"If you want to live, get the hell out of here," Bodie snapped. "This isn't about you."

"Not yet, it isn't, but unlike you, I'm not an idiot. I know you'll come after me so you can kill me and get my money. Well, it's not going to happen." Leland jabbed his index finger at Bodie. "Even if you manage to take me out, I changed my will. Jordana gets nothing."

All of this seemed like such a mundane conversation, considering there was a knife being held to her mother's throat, but Caroline welcomed it. As long as Leland kept Bodie's attention, then that meant Nash and she could look for a way to get Ruby and themselves out of here alive.

"You've known where Bodie was this whole time, haven't you?" Ruby asked Leland. "You knew and you didn't tell the cops."

Leland barely spared her a glance. "I'm trying to save my daughter, something I'm sure you understand."

"And you did that by helping Bodie escape," Ruby supplied. "Oh, he didn't know it was you, of course. You covered that up by hiring one of his former inmates. Barney Coltrain. Probably bribed the nurse, too, to take that throat punch. Then, I'm guessing you had a tracker either on the escape vehicle or something Barney gave Bodie. Like a phone."

Bingo.

Ruby had nailed it. Caroline could tell from Leland's expression. The man didn't deny any of it.

But Bodie had a reaction.

His face went hard with rage, and he moved fast. He hurled the knife at Leland, and it sliced right into his chest. In the same motion, Bodie whipped out another knife, this one identical to the other. Ruby moved, trying to get away, but Bodie put the knife to her throat again.

And this time, he cut her.

Caroline gasped as the blood started to ooze down her mother's throat.

"Bodie didn't hit the carotid artery," Nash told

her when she started to run to her mother. "He knows if he kills Ruby that he loses his human shield. Then, I kill the chickenshit coward where he stands."

Caroline forced those words to sink in. Forced herself to look at her mother. And she saw the slight shake of her head that Ruby gave her. A signal for her not to charge forward and try to help. It would be too dangerous of a move. Dangerous for her mother, for Nash, and for her.

And now, they had another big issue to deal with.

Leland was on the ground, his hands clutched around the hilt of the now bloody knife. He was alive, but Caroline didn't know for how long.

She wanted to use Oz to call for an ambulance, but that could be a dangerous move as well since Bodie might have his accomplice shoot the EMTs. Heck, Bodie might give the same order when Slade arrived so she prayed he took precautions.

Nash moved slightly, edging in front of Caroline. He probably wanted to make sure she stayed put.

"That's right," Bodie threw out there. "Put a leash on her, brother. Don't let her fight her own fight." He looked at Caroline and flashed her an oily smile. "Don't you want to have a go at me, darlin'?"

"I do," she admitted. "I want you dead."

Bodie cackled with laughter. "Sure you do. Well then, come on. Give it your best shot. Just me and you like it was in your dorm room. And if Nash decides to interfere, then I've got someone waiting to shoot him. I'm thinking a neck shot would work. Oh, the blood would spew just like it did when I shot Barney Coltrain."

Bodie glanced in the direction of the boats. Just a glance, but Nash must have seen it, too.

"Eddie's there," Nash remarked. "Not Jordana, though since you wouldn't have wanted to risk her to hear you call her a lap dog. Especially since she's more like a meal ticket."

Bodie's grin confirmed exactly that. "Eddie's a better choice for this op. He's a damn good shot, and he'll start firing on my say so." He moved his mouth to the communicator.

Maybe to give that go-ahead.

Once that was done, Eddie would start shooting and might indeed manage to kill them. Yes, they had on protective gear—her more than Nash—but she didn't want to risk it. She had to think of something now. She did.

But Nash beat her to it.

"You actually trust Eddie, a man who had an affair with your wife?" Nash threw out there.

Bodie's grin froze in place, and the cocky expression melted away. "What the fuck are you talking about?"

Ah, there it was. That barely controlled rage.

Caroline had gotten a full dose of that when he had attacked her. It was a risk to unleash it again, but anything they did was a risk, and she only hoped if Bodie completely lost it, that her mother could somehow manage to get out of the way. Ruby might not be in her prime any longer, but Caroline suspected she could deliver some blows if she got the chance.

"What the fuck are you talking about?" Bodie repeated.

"I'm talking about Jordana and Eddie having an affair. There's proof," Nash tacked onto that. "Want to see a picture that Maverick Ops uncovered? It's a really...revealing photo."

"It'll be Photoshopped," Bodie snarled, his words snapping out like gunshots. "A fake. Something you put together to rattle me and make me go after Eddie instead of Caroline."

"It's not, a fake" Leland managed to say. His voice was coated with pain, but he managed to sit up. Managed to dole out a sick smile to Bodie. "I've seen the photo myself. Jordana doesn't love you. You're like her version of slumming with the pool boy, asshole. You're her lap dog, and she played you."

Caroline doubted that last part was true. She'd seen Jordana's reaction to Bodie, and the woman seemed to love him. Or at least thought she did anyway. Leland might know that, too, but he'd probably wanted to fight back the only way he could.

With his words.

Those words seemed to sap Leland though of what was left of his energy. And his fight. He dropped his head back down on the ground.

Caroline didn't know how much time he had, but he needed medical help right away. That wasn't going to happen though until they dealt with Bodie.

"Ask Eddie," Nash pressed. "Ask him why he betrayed you by screwing around with your wife."

The rage skyrocketed in Bodie's eyes, and Caroline could see the debate Bodie was having with himself. "Enough of this," he yelled. "The cavalry will be here soon to try to help you. It's now or never, Caroline. Step up and take your punishment or Eddie—"

Bodie stopped. Just stopped. And he abruptly shifted his attention to his communicator. It was as if he couldn't focus on what he was doing until he got something else out of the way.

"Did you fuck her, Eddie? Did you?" Bodie shouted.

Caroline couldn't hear Eddie's response, but whatever it was, it clearly didn't please Bodie.

"You limp dick sonofabitch," Bodie snarled into the communicator. "You are a dead man."

That threat had barely left his mouth.

When the gunshots started.

CHAPTER EIGHTEEN

———— ☆ ————

Nash caught hold of Caroline, dragging her to the ground with him and trying to cover her as much as he could. That was hard to do, what with the bullets flying at them nonstop.

"You sonofabitch," Bodie yelled at the top of his lungs.

He, too, got down, darting in front of the limestone sign and using it for cover. Somehow, during all the maneuvering, he still managed to keep Ruby in a chokehold. Then again, Ruby might not have fought back since those bullets were being aimed at Bodie, it also meant they were also aimed at her. She had probably realized her best bet was to get out of the line of fire and then try to make her escape from Bodie.

From the corner of his eye, Nash saw both Bodie and Ruby hit hard on the ground, and Ruby grimaced in pain. Nash hoped one of those bullets hadn't hit her or that she'd broken something in the fall. While he was hoping, Nash added one more thing.

That Eddie wouldn't miss his target—Bodie—and shoot Ruby, Caroline, Leland or him instead.

Leland was especially vulnerable since he couldn't even seem to move to scramble out of the way. He was bleeding out, and there was nothing Nash could do to help him.

"Eddie," Caroline muttered. "He's doing this."

Yeah, he was. Nash was certain of it despite not actually being able to see the man. However, the shots were coming from one of the boats where Eddie had no doubt been hiding.

Waiting for Bodie's command to kill them.

Instead, Bodie had turned on his friend, and Eddie had likely decided it was shoot or be shot. No way would Bodie let him live after learning what'd happened between Jordana and him.

One of the bullets ricocheted off the limestone and slammed into the fence just above Caroline's and his heads. Nash figured that wouldn't be the last time that happened either. The giant slab of limestone was protecting Bodie, but it was putting Caroline and him in even more danger since those bits of rock could come flying at them like little missiles.

"Try to crawl back inside the gate," Nash instructed. At least that way she'd be further away from those ricochets.

Nash adjusted a little to give her room so she could start moving when another sound stopped him. Not the wail of sirens that he'd hoped to hear, but it was definitely a car engine, and as Leland had done, it was coming at them damn fast.

Nash cursed when he saw a dark blue car coming up the road. Not Slade. But rather Jordana. It wasn't her usual vehicle, but then the cops would have been looking for that.

She slammed on the brakes when she saw what was happening, but she didn't get down. Instead, she threw open her car door.

"Dad? Are you all right?" But then she shifted her attention to her husband. "Bodie," she shouted. "Get in. I can save you. I can save both Dad and you."

"Get back in your car, Jordana," Leland told her as he grimaced in pain. "You'll get killed out here."

She didn't listen. Instead, she volleyed glances at Bodie and her father, no doubt trying to decide what the hell to do.

Bodie turned, dragging Ruby so she was still his shield. But so he could also face his wife.

"Bitch, you cheated on me," Bodie snarled. "Kill her, Eddie," he shouted. "Do us both a favor and blow her brains out."

Jordana frantically shook her head. "I didn't. I, uh—" She screamed when a bullet skipped off the top of her car, barely missing her.

Still screaming and with Leland yelling for her to get down, she dived back in her car, and a moment later, Jordana came out with her own gun. "You told Eddie to kill me," she yelled at Bodie. "How could you do that? I'm your wife, and I've done everything for you."

"How could I do it? Easy peasy. Because, bitch, you cheated on me," Bodie fired back. "No one cheats on me. No one walks away from me."

Jordana's expression changed, and normally Nash would have welcomed the fury he saw there. But the fury wasn't for Bodie. No. It was projecting straight toward Caroline and him.

"You told him," Jordana spat out. "Caroline and you told him about that picture. That mistake."

The woman aimed her gun the same place she aimed that fury.

"You're going to pay for that," she growled. "You're both going to die."

Eddie thankfully stopped Jordana from firing a shot that could have indeed killed one of them. The man apparently had no loyalty toward the woman he'd had a one-off with because Eddie sent more rounds in Jordana's direction, forcing her to duck back down.

Nash helped Eddie out with that by firing a shot into Jordana's car. He didn't want to kill her, but he sure as hell would if she took aim at Caroline again.

"Try to get to the gate," Nash told Caroline once again.

But the shots shifted.

And not in a good direction.

Because Eddie was sending some gunfire their way now.

Shit. The idiot couldn't make up his mind

who he wanted to kill. The person he should be shooting at was Bodie. Because if Bodie made it out of here alive, he'd go straight for Eddie.

But Nash didn't intend for Bodie to walk away from this.

This ended here. It ended now. And it ended with his asshole brother dead, so he'd never be another threat to Caroline.

Nash scrambled back, trying to pin Caroline against the fence so his body would protect her. But she wasn't having any of that. She moved to his side, took aim at the boat and returned fire. Nash wasn't sure she hit Eddie, but it put a halt to his shooting. Probably because he had to duck down or risk being killed.

Jordana must have realized that Eddie was temporarily disabled because she came out of her car again. And, yeah, she took up where she'd left off by lifting her gun toward Caroline.

"Watch out," Ruby shouted, and she started to kick and shove, trying to put herself in between Caroline and Jordana.

Bodie obviously wasn't going to lose his leverage, and he hung on, giving Ruby another jab with the knife.

Nash didn't check to see how bad this cut was. He decided to do something about the enraged woman hellbent on killing them. When Jordana took aim.

So did Nash.

He didn't go for a kill shot, but he sent a bullet

right into her hand. She screamed again, and both her gun and the blood went flying. It was possible she'd lose a finger or two, but she sure as hell wouldn't be shooting with that hand any time soon.

"Jordana," Leland called out, and he yanked out the knife from his chest and began to crawl to his daughter.

Jordana sank down onto the ground, still screaming and cradling her injured hand. Nash hoped the woman didn't do anything stupid to make him shoot her again, but he had to be ready for that.

Ready for Bodie, too.

Caroline fired another shot at the boat, but then she gasped when she saw the fresh blood on her mother's neck. This second cut had likely still missed an artery, but it was deeper than the first. The blood was pouring.

And apparently so was Caroline's rage.

"You and me," Caroline snapped, and she pulled out her knife.

It took Nash a moment to realize she was issuing a challenge to Bodie. Hell. He didn't want this.

But apparently Bodie and she did.

Caroline got into a crouching position, and Bodie shifted his body so he'd be in a position to hurl his own knife right at Caroline. The asshole would no doubt aim for her throat.

And he might hit her, too.

That is, if Eddie didn't first.

Eddie must have realized he was no longer being shot at because he resumed firing. Not for long though.

"Enough of this shit," Nash snarled, and he pivoted, took aim at Eddie's head and blasted away.

Nash didn't miss.

Eddie dropped like a stone, and Nash immediately turned back to Bodie. But he was too late.

Hell, he was too late.

Bodie bashed Ruby against the limestone and shoved her aside. Without missing a beat, he tossed down his knife, whipped out a gun from his shoulder holster, and put his finger on the trigger.

The asshole coward was going to shoot Caroline, and she only had her knife to defend herself.

Nash took aim. But Caroline had already done that—with her knife. And she didn't hesitate. Just as she'd done in her studio with the target, she sent the knife flying. And it landed all right.

Directly into Bodie's chest.

Bodie went stock-still, and with his mouth open in shock, he looked down at all the blood as if he couldn't believe this was happening.

"You brought a knife to a gunfight," Bodie muttered, his eyes already glazing over.

And the last breath he'd ever take rattled from his throat as he crumpled to the ground.

CHAPTER NINETEEN

————— ☆ —————

Caroline sat in the open back of Slade's van with the really bad cup of coffee that one of the cops had given her.

She sat, sipped, and watched the first responders do their thing. Watched Nash, too, as he was giving his statement to one of the county deputies—something Caroline had already done.

Apparently, they'd given her top dibs in that department.

Maybe because she'd been the one to kill Bodie. Or it could have had something to do with her *on the edge* vibe she had no doubt been giving off. Added to that, she hadn't needed any medical attention like her mother, Jordana, and Leland.

Ruby was in the process of being interviewed as well by another deputy, while an EMT continued to clean and bandage the wounds on her neck. Like Nash, her mother kept glancing her way. Maybe making sure she wasn't about to lose it.

She wasn't.

Nowhere close to that.

But it was reasonable for them to think that she would what with her knife sticking out of Bodie's heart.

Slade was with the county sheriff and a team of CSIs, and they were likely discussing what needed to be searched and processed. Thankfully, not his house since the shitstorm hadn't happened there. But the harbor would definitely need to be checked out in case Eddie had left a stash of weapons there.

Watching a crime scene wasn't exactly old hat for her. Neither was killing a man. But as she saw the ME team lift Bodie's body into their van, she certainly wasn't feeling guilt. Or fear. Or panic. Or some tangled stew of all of those things.

No.

She was feeling relief. A Zen kind of sensation that might have been helped along with sheer exhaustion, spent adrenaline, and more of that relief. A whole mountain and ocean of it.

Bodie was dead. Stone cold dead, and part of her was glad she'd been the one to face him down.

And end him.

It felt like a full circle that had started when he'd attacked her eighteen years ago and finished right here with his blood soaking into the ground.

Of course, Jordana wasn't feeling much relief at the moment. She'd sobbed and wailed all while the EMT's were treating her wounded hand, and she was continuing the sobbing and wailing now that the cops were carting her away to jail. Caroline had heard the cops talking about charging her as an accomplice in Barney Coltrain's murder. She wouldn't get off with just a slap on the wrist for that.

Leland wasn't faring much better than this daughter. One set of EMTs had immediately taken him to the hospital. But if and when he recovered, he'd be facing charges, too, since he'd not only helped Bodie escape so he could murder him, Leland had also obstructed justice.

No charges for Eddie, though. Like Bodie, he was being carried off in a body bag. Again, Caroline couldn't muster up even a little sadness over that. The man had been willing to kill them.

And for what?

To help a sick bastard carry through on an old grudge against her? A grudge that Bodie had started when he'd stabbed her. Yeah, Eddie wasn't going to get any sympathy from her.

She looked up when Ruby started her way. Her mother wasn't her usual put-together self. Probably because of the blood on her clothes and her disheveled hair.

Caroline thought she'd never looked better.

Then again, that Zen thing was likely coloring her view. Her mother was alive, and one wrong flick of the knife, and she might not have been.

"How's your coffee?" her mother asked. She was drinking her own cup of the nasty brew and grimacing with each sip.

"I think they soaked old tires in stagnant water

and called it coffee." Caroline moved over a bit so Ruby could sit next to her. "Are you all right?"

She nodded. "Just scratches. I know when some men say that, it's really a gash, but in my case, it isn't." She sipped more coffee, and like Caroline, her gaze was fixed on Nash.

Speaking of *never looking better*, Nash fit into that category as well. The combat warrior/ guardian angel. With an amazing face. And butt. Yes, that butt was rather superior.

As if Nash had known she was thinking of him, he turned, and their gazes collided. A thousand things seemed to pass between them. And Caroline liked that very much. That even without words, they were connected.

"I'm sorry," Ruby said, re-snagging Caroline's attention. "I shouldn't have let Bodie get to me so he could use me to draw you out."

Caroline glanced at her. Frowned. Then, huffed. "Apology not accepted. Because it's not needed," she added when she saw her mother's fallen expression. "He was going to come after me one way or another. If he hadn't used you, it would have been someone else. Someone who might not have been able to survive."

Her mother made a slight sound of agreement, but Caroline thought that agreement would grow by leaps and bounds when she gave it more thought. Yes, Ruby was banged up, but she was mentally and physically tough. This wouldn't break her the way it would have done to someone else.

"My life flashed before my eyes," her mother went on while sipping more coffee and grimacing from the taste. "Never happened to me before."

"Oh, and what did you see?" she asked, and because Ruby's tone suddenly seemed so deep and intense, Caroline found herself drinking more of the sludge as well.

You." Ruby leaned over and brushed a kiss on Caroline's forehead. "My baby. My daughter. A woman capable of, well, anything. Not to make light of this, but you kicked his ass."

"I did," Caroline verified.

"How'd you learn to throw a knife like that?" she asked.

"Training and lots of practice. I've gone through eleven wooden targets over the years." She paused. "Somehow, I always knew it would come down to him and me, and I wanted to be ready this time."

"Oh, you were ready. So ready that I should offer you a job at Maverick Ops."

Caroline shook her head and figured Ruby was joking. Maybe not, though. But that kind of work wasn't for her.

"We haven't talked like this in a long time," her mother continued a moment later. "It feels like some kind of turning point."

"It is. Forgive and forget," Caroline muttered. Then, she shrugged. "Well, forgive anyway. I, uh, think what I was feeling about the attack eighteen years ago got tangled up with feelings of Dad dying. Of you not being there. It became that barrier between us. Maybe this is the post-adrenaline junk talking, but I think it's time for that barrier to come down."

She looked at her mother and was surprised to see tears in her eyes. Surprised, too, to feel them in her own.

Ruby smiled, leaned over and kissed her on the forehead again. "Barrier is down. Maybe that means you can come for dinner." Her mother paused a heartbeat. "And bring Nash."

Now, Caroline smiled. "I think that's a nice invitation to what would be a very uncomfortable meal for him. I'll bring him, though if you promise not to glare at him for sleeping with the boss' daughter."

Oops. She hadn't meant to blurt that out. But judging from Ruby's casual lift of the shoulder, she had already known.

Of course, she had. She was Ruby Maverick.

Ruby sipped more coffee and spoke with her gaze now fixed on Nash. "You're in love with him?"

Since she'd already spilled about the sex, Caroline continued with the truth. "Yeah, I am."

Once again, her mother did not seem the least bit surprised.

"Does he know?" Ruby asked.

Nash's ESP must have kicked up because he glanced at her again while he finished his talk with the cop. He started toward her, looking far between that of a Greek god of hotness could have managed.

"He doesn't know I'm in love with him. Not yet," Caroline added. "Are you going to give us your blessing?"

Ruby leaned in and whispered, "You've always had it." She gave her another kiss, on the cheek this time and got up. "I'll give you two a moment while I call for a ride home."

"We can give you a lift," Nash offered when he heard what she said.

Ruby shook her head. "I think you two need some time to discuss things." She brushed her hand on Nash's arm. "Are you okay?" she tacked onto that, glancing at the ME van that was driving away with Bodie's body.

"I'm okay if Caroline is," he said.

"Then, we're all okay," Caroline assured him.

"Good," her mother muttered. "The mission was a success. Take some downtime," she added and began to make her way toward Slade.

That "all okay" was close enough to the truth anyway. Once they'd had that downtime, it'd be the full truth. And once she told him that part about being in love with him.

She'd felt bold and invincible when she spilled to her mother about that. But now it occurred to her that Nash might not feel the same way as she did. Heck, this could have just been the job to him, and he might—

He took hold of her shoulders, pulled her

to him, and kissed her. It was long, hot, and wonderful. The kind of kiss that ignited flames and gave a promise of things to come.

"So," he said when he finally pulled back. He'd left her breathless, dizzy, and wanting a whole lot more. "Slade says I should take you back into the lake house, that I should put you in the hot tub, and…well, I'd rather not spell out his suggestions, but they're really good ones."

Yes, definitely a lot of promise.

"Can we go now?" she asked.

"Absolutely." He helped her out of the van and hooked his arm around her, already leading her through the gates to where he'd left his SUV. "Did you work out some things with your mom?"

"I did. Forgive and forgive. The forgetting might kick in a little later," she tacked onto that. "Oh, and she wants us to come for dinner."

Nash's head whipped toward her, and she laughed at the brief look of panic on his incredible face. "You can say no."

He helped her onto the seat of the SUV but kept her facing toward him. This put them at eye level. Mouth level, too.

"I don't want to say no," he assured her.

"You mean that?" she had to ask.

"I do. I, uh, think your mother should get used to seeing us together."

Oh, she liked the sound of that. "Does that mean because we'll start dating?"

"Among other things." He kissed her.

She liked that, too. A lot. And the kiss made her feel so needy that she had to fight the feeling just to say what she needed him to hear.

"I don't want to be a job for you," she started.

She groaned. Bad start. So, she regrouped.

"I want you in my life," Caroline said on her second attempt. "And in my bed."

He grinned. "That's a good place to be except you don't have a bed so it'll have to be mine."

"Sounds perfect." The location didn't matter. This was all about the company. "So, sex, dating—"

"I'm in love with you, Caroline," he interrupted. "You're probably going to say it's too soon for me to feel that way, but it isn't. I swear, it's the real deal, and—"

"I'm in love with you, too," she interrupted right back. "Head over heels, crazy in love with you."

Nash stared at her. And stared. Then, that slow grin spread over his mouth. A grin he shared with her when he leaned in and kissed her.

All of his kisses were amazing, but it felt as if he'd put some extra heat in this one. It was perfect. And once again, she felt as if it had sealed some kind of deal.

A deal she wanted very much with Nash.

"Let's go to the hot tub," Nash whispered with his mouth against her ear. "And get started on that downtime."

★☆★

EXCERPT FROM LONE STAR WITNESS

Book 5 of the Hard Justice, Texas Series

PROLOGUE

——————— ☆ ———————

The baseball bat slammed into Slade McKenna's back. Hard. It was a bone-rattling blow that nearly brought him to his knees.

Nearly.

It was bad luck for his attackers that he managed to stay on his feet, dodge another whack from the bat, and in a blink assess the shitstorm that was already on him.

There were three men, all about his size—big and beefy—and they had pretty much surrounded him in the dark parking lot of the seedy Texas Trails Motel. One was behind him armed with that damn metal baseball bat. Another to his right with a Bowie knife that he was holding in a such a way that let Slade know he knew how to use it.

And the third, straight ahead, had a gun.

It was a cheap assed Saturday Night Special. But cheap ass could still kill.

Take out the biggest threat first.

That's what Slade had been trained to do, first in the military and now in his job as an elite security specialist at Maverick Ops. The blow from the bat hadn't screwed up his moves or slowed him down. Hallelujah on that because he charged forward in what he called the pissed off bull gets the matador.

Slade rammed his head straight into the gun holder's throat while giving him a punch to the gut and kneeing him in the balls. All in one fluid motion. Some would probably consider that last part dirty fighting. And it was. But these dicks had attacked him, so bring on the dirty and amp it up a notch.

He kicked the gun out of the dick's hand and spun around. And got whacked again with the sonofabitching bat. This time, the blow landed on his side, and he could have sworn that he heard his ribs cursing him.

Slade was doing some cursing, too, and he dodged attempted blow number three by grabbing the bat and giving Dick Two a little of his own medicine. He caught hold of the bat and shoved it as hard as he could into the guy's face. Blood spewed, and there was the satisfying sound of cartilage breaking in his nose. Even with that, the idiot tried to come at Slade, so he repeated what he'd done to Dick One.

Head butt to the throat, gut punch, and a kick to the balls with his steel toes combat boots.

He went down.

Just as Dick Three lashed out with his knife.

Slade felt the slice of the blade. Felt the pain shoot through him as if controlled by an electric fence. It hurt. Bad. But again, Slade shook it off enough to dodge another attempted stab.

He ducked to the side and didn't waste a second coming right back. Right at Dick Three. No kick to the balls this time. Slade went old school and gave him a right hook, followed by a left, then another right, this time to the side of his head. Before tonight, that was a combo that had been one hundred percent effective.

And it apparently still was.

The guy's eyes glazed over, and he dropped like a stone.

With all three down, Slade finally drew his gun, something he hadn't had the chance to do when they'd ambushed him.

"I will shoot you in the balls if you move or try to come at me again," he warned them, and he made sure there was no hesitation in his voice. No bluffing tone. Because he would do just that.

"Spock," he said to his artificial intelligence security app on his phone. So named as a tribute to his late mom. "Call the cops. And an ambulance," he added. Not for himself but for Dick Three, who likely had a concussion.

Since all three were on the ground and were moaning, writhing in pain or making other annoying sounds, Slade kept his gun aimed at them and backed toward the door to room 112. It was cracked open enough for him to see the woman peering out.

For him to see the terror etched on her face and

in her eyes.

"You're safe," he told her just as Spock came back with a reply.

"Responders are on the way," the app said in its blank emotional tone. "And you just got a voicemail."

Slade was about to tell Spock that any and all voicemails or calls could wait until he got this woman home.

Then, Spock added something that changed everything. Spock said her name. Just her name. And Slade knew.

He needed to get to her fast.

———— ☆ ————

ABOUT THE HARD JUSTICE TEXAS SERIES:

★☆★

The Maverick Ops team members are former military and cops who assist law enforcement in cold cases and hot investigations where lives are on the line. Their specialty is rescuing kidnapped victims, tracking down killers and protecting those in the path of danger. Maverick Ops is known for doing what it does best--delivering some hard justice.

★☆★

ABOUT THE
AUTHOR:

★☆★

Former Air Force Captain Delores Fossen is a USA Today, Amazon and Publisher's Weekly bestselling author of over 150 books. She's received the Booksellers Best Award for Best Romantic Suspense and the Romantic Times Reviewers Choice Award. In addition, she's had nearly a hundred short stories and articles published in national magazines. You can contact the author through her webpage at www.deloresfossen.com.

★☆★

HARD JUSTICE, TEXAS SERIES BOOKS BY DELORES FOSSEN:

Lone Star Rescue (book 1)

Lone Star Showdown (book 2)

Lone Star Payback (book 3)

Lone Star Protector (book 4)

Lone Star Witness (book 5)

Lone Star Target (book 6)

Lone Star Secrets (book 7)

———————— ★☆★ ————————

Visit deloresfossen.com for more titles
and release dates. Also sign up for Delores'
newsletter at https://www.deloresfossen.com/
contactnewsletter.html

★☆★

OTHER BOOKS BY DELORES FOSSEN:

Appaloosa Pass Ranch

1 - Lone Wolf Lawman (Nov-2015)

2 - Taking Aim at the Sheriff (Dec-2015)

3 - Trouble with a Badge (Apr-2016)

4 - The Marshal's Justice (May-2016)

5 - Six-Gun Showdown (Aug-2016)

6 - Laying Down the Law (Sep-2016)

Blue River Ranch

1 - Always a Lawman (Dec-2017)

2 - Gunfire on the Ranch (Jan-2018)

3 - Lawman From Her Past (Mar-2018)

4 - Roughshod Justice (Apr-2018)

Coldwater, Texas

1 - Lone Star Christmas (Sep-2018)

1.5 - Lone Star Midnight (Jan-2019)

2 - Hot Texas Sunrise (Mar-2019)

2.5 - Texas at Dusk (Jun-2019)

3 - Sweet Summer Sunset (Jun-2019)

4 - A Coldwater Christmas (Sep-2019)

Cowboy Brothers in Arms

1 - Heart Like a Cowboy (Dec-2023)

2 - Always a Maverick (May-2024)

3 – Cowboying Up (working title) 2024

Five Alarm Babies

1 - Undercover Daddy (May-2007)

2 - Stork Alert // Whose Baby? (Aug-2007)

3 - The Christmas Clue (Nov-2007)

4 - Newborn Conspiracy (Feb-2008)

5 - The Horseman's Son // The Cowboy's Son (Mar-2008)

Last Ride, Texas

1 - Spring at Saddle Run (May-2021)

2 - Christmas at Colts Creek (Nov-2021)

3 - Summer at Stallion Ridge (Apr-2022)

3.5 - Second Chance at Silver Springs (Oct-2022)

4 - Mornings at River's End Ranch (Dec-2022)

4.5 - Breaking Rules at Nightfall Ranch (Feb-2023)

5 - A Texas Kind of Cowboy (Mar-2023)

6 - Twilight at Wild Springs (Jul-2023)

The Law in Lubbock County

1 - Sheriff in the Saddle (Jul-2022)

2 - Maverick Justice (Aug-2022)

3 - Lawman to the Core (Jan-2023)

4 - Spurred to Justice (Jan-2023)

The Lawmen of Silver Creek Ranch

1 - Grayson (Nov-2011)

2 - Dade (Dec-2011)

3 - Nate (Jan-2012)

4 - Kade (Jul-2012)

5 - Gage (Aug-2012)

6 - Mason (Sep-2012)

7 - Josh (Apr-2014)

8 - Sawyer (May-2014)

9 - Landon (Nov-2016)

10 - Holden (Mar-2017)

11 - Drury (Apr-2017)

12 - Lucas (May-2017)

The Lawmen of McCall Canyon

1 - Cowboy Above the Law (Aug-2018)

2 - Finger on the Trigger (Sep-2018)

3 - Lawman with a Cause (Jan-2019)

4 - Under The Cowboy's Protection (Feb-2019)

Lone Star Ridge

1 - Tangled Up in Texas (Feb-2020)

1.5 - That Night in Texas (May-2020)

2 - Chasing Trouble in Texas (Jun-2020)

2.5 - Hot Summer in Texas (Sep-2020)

3 - Wild Nights in Texas (Oct-2020)

3.5 - Whatever Happens in Texas (Jan-2021)

4 - Tempting in Texas (Feb-2021)

5 - Corralled in Texas (Mar-2022)

Longview Ridge Ranch

1 - Safety Breach (Dec-2019)

2 - A Threat to His Family (Jan-2020)

3 - Settling an Old Score (Aug-2020)

4 - His Brand of Justice (Sep-2020)

The Marshals of Maverick County

1 - The Marshal's Hostage (May-2013)

2 - One Night Standoff (Jun-2013)

3 - Outlaw Lawman (Jul-2013)

4 - Renegade Guardian (Nov-2013)

5 - Justice Is Coming (Dec-2013)

6 - Wanted (Jan-2014)

McCord Brothers

0.5 - What Happens on the Ranch (Jan-2016)

1 - Texas on My Mind (Feb-2016)

1.5 - Cowboy Trouble (May-2016)

2 - Lone Star Nights (Jun-2016)

2.5 - Cowboy Underneath It All (Aug-2016)

3 - Blame It on the Cowboy (Oct-2016)

Mercy Ridge Lawmen

1 - Her Child to Protect (May-2021)

2 - Safeguarding the Surrogate (Jul-2021)

3 - Targeting the Deputy (Dec-2021)

4 - Pursued by the Sheriff (Jan-2022)

Mustang Ridge

1 - Christmas Rescue at Mustang Ridge (Dec-2012)

2 - Standoff at Mustang Ridge (Jan-2013)

Silver Creek Lawmen: Second Generation

1 - Targeted in Silver Creek (Jul-2023)

2 - Maverick Detective Dad (Aug-2023)

3 - Last Seen in Silver Creek (Sep-2023)

4 - Marked For Revenge (Oct-2023)

Sweetwater Ranch

1 - Maverick Sheriff (Sep-2014)

2 - Cowboy Behind the Badge (Oct-2014)

3 - Rustling Up Trouble (Nov-2014)

4 - Kidnapping in Kendall County (Dec-2014)

5 - The Deputy's Redemption (Mar-2015)

6 - Reining in Justice (Apr-2015)

7 - Surrendering to the Sheriff (Jul-2015)

8 - A Lawman's Justice (Aug-2015)

Texas Maternity Hostages

1 - The Baby's Guardian (May-2010)

2 - Daddy Devastating (Jun-2010)

3 - The Mommy Mystery (Jul-2010)

Texas Maternity: Labor and Delivery

1 - Savior in the Saddle (Nov-2010)

2 - Wild Stallion (Dec-2010)

3 - The Texas Lawman's Last Stand (Jan-2011)

Texas Paternity

1 - Security Blanket (Oct-2008)

2 - Branded By The Sheriff (Jan-2009)

3 - Expecting Trouble (Feb-2009)

4 - Secret Delivery (Mar-2009)

5 - Christmas Guardian (Oct-2009)

A Wrangler's Creek Novel

1 - Those Texas Nights (Jan-2017)

2 - No Getting Over a Cowboy (Apr-2017)

3 - Branded as Trouble (Jul-2017)

4 - Lone Star Cowboy (Nov-2016)

5 - One Good Cowboy (Feb-2017)

6 - Just Like a Cowboy (May-2017)

7 - Texas-Sized Trouble (Jan-2018)

8 - Lone Star Blues (Apr-2018)

9 - The Last Rodeo (Jul-2018)

10 - Cowboy Dreaming (Dec-2017)

11 - Cowboy Heartbreaker (Mar-2018)

12 - Cowboy Blues (May-2018)

Daddy Corps

G.I. Cowboy (Apr-2011)

Ice Lake

Cold Heat (Jan-2012)

Kenner County Crime Unit

She's Positive (Jul-2009)

Men on a Mission

Marching Orders (Mar-2003)

Shivers

20 - His to Possess (Oct-2014)

The Silver Star of Texas

Trace Evidence In Tarrant County // For Justice and Love (Feb-2007)

Questioning The Heiress (Jul-2008)

Shotgun Sheriff (Feb-2010)

Top Secret Babies

Mommy Under Cover (Feb-2005)

Made in the USA
Coppell, TX
28 August 2024

36576803R10125